FUJINO OMORI

ILLUSTRATION BY
KIYOTAKA HAIMURA

CHARACTER DESIGN BY
SUZUHITO YASUDA

Riveria looked troubled by the request, but—

"U-
th
Could you tell me a bit more about how Miss Aiz used to be?"

IS IT WRONG TO TRY TO PICK UP GIRLS IN A DUNGEON? ON THE SIDE

Sword Oratoria

CONTENTS

© Kiyotaka Haimura

Finally, the mountain of corpses was complete.

Standing in the center of the beasts' grave was a bloodstained golden-haired, golden-eyed girl.

"...Done."

GARETH LANDROCK:
A veteran dwarf soldier and the oldest member of *Loki Familia*.

AIZ WALLENSTEIN:
A girl who joined *Loki Familia*. Hailed as the Doll Princess.

© Kiyotaka Haimura

Sword Oratoria

Is it WRONG to TRY to PICK UP GIRLS iN A DUNGEON? ON THE SiDE

VOLUME 9

FUJINO OMORI

ILLUSTRATION BY
KIYOTAKA HAIMURA

CHARACTER DESIGN BY
SUZUHITO YASUDA

IS IT WRONG TO TRY TO PICK UP GIRLS IN A DUNGEON?
ON THE SIDE: SWORD ORATORIA, Volume 9
FUJINO OMORI

Translation by Dale DeLucia
Cover art by Kiyotaka Haimura

DUNGEON NI DEAI WO MOTOMERU NO WA MACHIGATTEIRUDAROUKA GAIDEN
SWORD ORATORIA vol. 9
Copyright © 2017 Fujino Omori
Illustration copyright © Kiyotaka Haimura
Original Character Design © Suzuhito Yasuda
All rights reserved.
Original Japanese edition published in 2017 by SB Creative Corp.
This English edition is published by arrangement with SB Creative Corp., Tokyo, in care of Tuttle-Mori Agency, Inc., Tokyo.

English translation © 2019 by Yen Press, LLC

Yen On
1290 Avenue of the Americas
New York, NY 10104

Visit us at yenpress.com
facebook.com/yenpress
twitter.com/yenpress
yenpress.tumblr.com
instagram.com/yenpress

First Yen On Edition: June 2019

Yen On is an imprint of Yen Press, LLC.
The Yen On name and logo are trademarks of Yen Press, LLC.

The publisher is not responsible for websites (or their content) that are not owned by the publisher.

Library of Congress Cataloging-in-Publication Data
Names: Ōmori, Fujino, author. | Haimura, Kiyotaka, 1973– illustrator. | Yasuda, Suzuhito, designer.
Title: Is it wrong to try to pick up girls in a dungeon? on the side: sword oratoria / story by Fujino Omori; illustration by Kiyotaka Haimura; original design by Suzuhito Yasuda.
Other titles: Danjon ni deai wo motomeru no wa machigatteirudarouka gaiden sword oratoria. English.
Description: New York, NY: Yen On, 2016– | Series: Is it wrong to try to pick up girls in a dungeon? on the side: sword oratoria
Identifiers: LCCN 2016023729 | ISBN 9780316315333 (v. 1 : pbk.) | ISBN 9780316318167 (v. 2 : pbk.) | ISBN 9780316318181 (v. 3 : pbk.) | ISBN 9780316318228 (v. 4 : pbk.) | ISBN 9780316442503 (v. 5 : pbk.) | ISBN 9780316442527 (v. 6 : pbk.) | ISBN 9781975302863 (v. 7 : pbk.) | ISBN 9781975327798 (v. 8 : pbk.) | ISBN 9781975327811 (v. 9 : pbk.)
Subjects: CYAC: Fantasy.
Classification: LCC PZ7.1.O54 Isg 2016 Y DDC [Fic]—dc23
LC record available at https://lccn.loc.gov/2016023729

ISBNs: 978-1-9753-2781-1 (paperback)
978-1-9753-2782-8 (ebook)

1 3 5 7 9 10 8 6 4 2

LSC-C

Printed in the United States of America

VOLUME 9

FUJINO OMORI

ILLUSTRATION BY **KIYOTAKA HAIMURA**
CHARACTER DESIGN BY **SUZUHITO YASUDA**

RECOLLECTIONS OF AN ELF

Гэта казка іншага свету

памяць фею

There was a certain state known as the Kingdom of Rakia.

It was nominally a militant monarchy located in the western part of the continent, but in actuality, it was headed by the deity Ares and built up by his followers—*Ares Familia.* All the kingdom's soldiers and military personnel had received a Blessing and since time immemorial would constantly wage war at the behest of their god's divine will. Their armies had a history of expanding by force, invading other cities and countries.

And now they were embarking on a new military expedition.

—The Kingdom of Rakia's army was marching on Orario.

The nation of warmongers had pointed its spear at the very center of the world. Crimson banners fluttered and countless boots thundered as they steadily advanced on the giant walls protecting the city.

The Guild drafted a mission, dispatching several familias based in the city to intercept the invading army. *Loki Familia* was one of those summoned.

The curtain rose on the war between the invaders and the adventurers.

"Gyaaaaaaaaaaaaaaaa?!"

But—

"Captain, Gareth is blowing away the unit of knights by himself according to plan."

"Tell him to keep intercepting them like that. I'm sorry to work him so hard, but they still have reinforcements coming."

"Captain! I busted up three of the squads that were trying to retreat like you ordered!"

"Good job, Tione. But you're supposed to be relaying my orders, not personally carrying them out."

The battle had turned into a one-sided assault launched by Orario's forces.

On a plain far to the east of the city, a never-ending stream of screams echoed across the battlefield. From their camp overlooking the battlefront, members of *Loki Familia* watched as the Rakian army was put to rout. Thanks to its proximity to the Dungeon, Orario had gathered the world's strongest adventurers. In this age of gods where quality surpassed quantity, when Rakia's soldiers were only Level 3s at best, they had no chance of gaining the upper hand. While their enemies struggled, Orario's adventurers appeared unfazed, even bored.

"We've got a bunch of issues popping up thanks to the Evils, so why is Rakia bugging us now?"

"Our troubles are obviously not a problem in their eyes."

"I guess it's like our goddess always says about the timing being bad."

Considering that a hostile nation had invaded, this was technically an emergency. As one of the city's strongest groups, *Loki Familia* was forced to take part in the defense. The flags with the trickster's emblem that currently served as their battle standard were clearly sapping the enemy's will to fight whenever they saw one.

Deployed as messengers, Tiona, the catgirl Anakity, and the human Narfi exchanged strained laughs and sighs as they carefully moved among the various groups.

"—*Fusillade Fallarica!*"

On the main battlefront, countless fiery missiles streaked across the field.

Lefiya held a staff in both hands. Exactly as planned, she loosed a wide-range bombardment spell on the enemy formation that was advancing on them.

A thunderous boom sounded right before a crater appeared in the ground, sending soldiers and horses flying. The opposing army was already on the verge of collapse after a single blast. Everyone, from the enemy soldiers to the various familias from Orario comprising the rest of the temporary alliance, shuddered at the sight of the elf standing on the top of the hill.

"Lefiya, you're overdoing it. The goal is to force them to retreat. At this rate, you'll totally wipe them out."

"S-sorry, Miss Alicia…Maybe it's because we are always fighting monsters in the Dungeon, but it's somewhat hard to hold back…"

"Let's try harder next time…We're moving on now, as the captain ordered."

Alicia, the Level-4 elf adventurer, corrected the girl's timing on her spell. Lefiya clutched her staff and hung her head at the older elf's look of disappointment. Riviera was too powerful, so she was working behind the scenes while Lefiya's attacks exploded around the battlefield.

It was a raw demonstration of quality over quantity.

A single skilled mage had—with a single spell—scattered a hundred units.

To the Rakian soldiers, it was a living nightmare.

"Aghhh, Commander! That pink elf from Orario is coming this way! Gah…She's Concurrent Castiiing!"

"Retreat! Retreeeat!!! We can't hold!"

A Level-3 fast-response weapon platform on legs. That day, the pink elf became a symbol of terror for the *Ares Familia* soldiers as she dashed around the battlefield raining immense magic attacks on them.

"Damn you, Orario scum!! Stand and fight! Stop waddling around and blasting magic all over! Does no one in this forsaken city understand the beauty of proper battle?!"

"Lord Ares…A mob of adventurers who resort to sneak attacks and schemes obviously wouldn't know anything about the art of war. Besides, didn't we also prepare several artillery units with the intent of using them for a trap on our enemies?"

"Wh-what's with that accusing tone of voice, Marius?! I'll have you beheaded!"

"—Reporting! Our front lines have completely collapsed due to *Loki Familia*'s insane mag—Due to the Thousand Elf! We've nearly been wiped out!"

"Gah! M-Marius! Do something!"

"Very well. Have all the troops retreat. We're withdrawing from this position."

The magical explosions were already sending tremors through the Rakian army's base camp. While the God of War's bellows reverberated in the luxurious tent, the first prince of Rakia who served as his executive officer began issuing orders in a practiced manner, or perhaps it was better described as *resigned*.

Finn had ordered his familia to show Lefiya off as the successor to Riveria, the city's strongest magic user, and the Thousand Elf's reputation grew by leaps and bounds after the battle. The news even made waves among the familias in Orario.

Of course, he also wanted to encourage the growth of her magic abilities, but his ulterior motive was to exploit anything he could to solidify *Loki Familia*'s position, no matter how small. How this led to the young elven girl catching the attention of a certain magic country will have to be a story for another time.

"Lefiya's really lettin' 'em have it."

The patron gods of the various familias that had been summoned to defend Orario were gathered atop a hill far from the battlefield. Despite the distance, they could still observe the merciless onslaught as Lefiya's magic savaged the opposing army. The snot- and tear-filled cries of the enemy reverberated across the landscape.

Loki slumped back down into her chair, losing interest.

"Tedious, isn't it…?"

"I've got bigger fish to fry, ya know…"

Loki's response was natural, given how she had postponed her familia's search for the key to Knossos due to current events, which she considered to be a colossal waste of time. Next to her was Freya, the silver-haired Goddess of Beauty, who was being waited on by a follower she had brought along. She also didn't know what to do with herself.

This was just another duty required of the city's two strongest factions. If they hadn't made an appearance on the battlefield, the Rakian army would have let it go to their heads, which left these two familias no choice but to be front and center. Loki sighed again, having long since lost count of how many times this had already happened.

Rakia had picked fights with Orario before, suffering losses every time. The main impetus for the attack this time was likely because Ares was looking to satisfy his long-standing grudge and had yet to learn his lesson. Incidentally, this was their sixth attempt to invade, as discussed at Denatus.

"Ares, ya dumbass, if you can see the difference in strength, then don't attack in the first place! What a joke."

Loki mumbled her complaint while stifling a yawn.

"That girl's actually become half-decent..."

"That's rare, Bete. I'm surprised to hear you praising someone you normally call a weakling."

"Screw you," the werewolf muttered. Riveria wore a half smile as she watched the younger elf's countless spells arcing down around the plains.

They were near a patch of woods away from the main battlefield. Taking Aiz, Bete, and a small group of familia members, Riveria was leading the counterattack against the Rakian army, crushing any detachments of soldiers that were trying to sneak around. All their targets had been knocked out, and the rest of Riveria's party was busy tying them up.

Observing Lefiya's performance alongside Bete, Riveria began to comment.

"She still has a ways to go...Of course I mean in her technique, too, but right now Lefiya's heart is wavering."

"...Huh?"

"She's impatient."

Riveria was also a spellcaster, meaning she noticed flaws in the girl's craft that Bete missed.

Watching the sweaty elf in the distance who weaved spell after spell, Riveria was reminded of someone else, and her gaze narrowed.

"The more you hurry, the less room you have to breathe...and the more you hurt yourself...That girl was like that, too," Riveria said to herself under her breath.

"What girl? You mean Aiz?"

Her murmur did not escape the ears of the animal person next to her. Bete glanced over at the golden-haired, golden-eyed girl keeping watch a short distance away.

In response, Riveria simply changed the topic.

"Whatever happened to Lena Tully after all that? She seemed awfully attached to—"

"—Can it! Don't you dare bring that up, hag!"

The effect was immediate as Bete started hollering. Instantly fed up, the werewolf stormed off to escape further discussion.

"…"

Now that she was alone, Riveria looked at Aiz, the commotion of the battlefield rolling over them in waves.

The girl was doing her job while watching the surroundings with interest. A small bird chirped, paying her no mind as it descended, landing on her finger as she tilted her head in curiosity. It was as though the bird had been called to her by the wind, entranced by a spirit of the element.

This nature, this landscape, this fragrance did not exist in Orario. They were all fresh and new to the girl. In fact, even counting the time in Meren, she had been outside the Labyrinth City only a handful of times—she had no memories of anything beyond that confined area.

For Aiz, this view of the outside world is unknown.

"There are so many things I still have yet to teach her…"

Aiz Wallenstein's everything lies inside those walls.

Riveria murmured as she gazed at the girl's figure.

Softly, she pushed at the door of recollections inside her mind.

Yes.

She could remember it even now.

When she had first grasped her sword.

The young girl was crying.

Her voice raised and throat rasping as tears streamed down her cheeks.

First, she stared up at the gray sky.

Then she stared around the room she had been brought to.

Her tiny chest kept quivering.

A flood of emotions overwhelmed her, merging together inside until she couldn't even tell what she was sad about anymore. She couldn't hear the voices of the people incessantly calling out to her. Fragments of her meaningless sobs fell to the floor, leaving countless stains. The hole that had been torn open in her heart dragged her into a darkness that felt unbearably cold.

The sun rose; the sun set.

Again. And again. And again. Time kept moving without her.

No matter how much she cried, the world refused to change.

The people she loved would not hug her anymore.

Her irreplaceable happiness would never come back.

Her cries went unanswered.

Her *hero* didn't appear.

"Wouldn't it be nice if you met a wonderful partner, too."

Her mother's words were nothing more than a dream.

"I hope that someday, you find a hero—your hero."

Her father's words were just a fairy tale.

A hero who would save her had never existed in the first place.

The instant she understood that in the back of her mind, she felt her heart freeze over.

An eternal wall of ice that would never melt guarded it.

And so.

When her throat was too sore to sob and she had no more tears to shed, she spoke.

The young girl had lost her innocence.

All emotion vanished from her expression, leaving her face like a doll's and her eyes like swords as she pleaded.

"I want power."

The crimson-haired goddess, the prum hero, the great dwarf warrior, and the high elf mage. As they sorrowfully gazed down upon her, she made her request.

The girl's small hands drew the sword that had been thrust into her heart.

That was the moment the Sword Princess was born.

A SCENE AT THE CAMP

Гэта казка іншага сям

Аднаактовы ў лагеры

"Guahhh…"

Lefiya was listless.

She still had Mind to spare, but her body was exhausted from all the Concurrent Casting.

"Good work, Lefiya!"

"You were a huge help out there. Here, dinner."

"Ah, thank you…"

Tiona and Tione encouraged her.

A moonlit night had fallen. *Loki Familia*'s camp had been set up at the edge of the plain, a position that would let them stare down at the Rakian army. *Ares Familia*'s encampment was visible in the distance, but the surrounding tents lit by campfires and magic-stone lanterns all belonged to Orario's familias.

Lefiya had been maneuvering around the battlefield to launch her attacks since the very start of the fight. All according to Finn's plan. She had satisfactorily fulfilled her role by providing mobile fire support, blowing holes in the enemy's defenses and their strategy as well as training her Concurrent Casting ability.

"But really, you were amazing today, Lefiya! As your roommate, I'm proud."

"What are you feeling proud for? Well, this isn't exactly making the best of a less-than-ideal situation, but I think the captain probably intended to use the battle to put Lefiya on display for everyone in and outside Orario."

"You mean as 'the successor of the city's strongest mage,' right?"

"Oooh, I get it. Like announcing to the world that *Loki Familia*'s still got it. Telling everyone 'check out our future first-tier adventurer.'"

Some of the familia's girls were sitting down together. Lefiya's roommate, the magic user Elfie; the other human Narfi; the catgirl Anakity;

and the elf Alicia all chimed in as Lefiya quietly sipped at her stew, looking down.

"What future first-tier adventurer?...I'm nowhere near that yet. I didn't even manage to do everything the captain asked without messing up today..."

"You performed perfectly today, Lefiya. You did your job just fine."

"But I couldn't completely control my magic; the spells kept getting too big...And I think I accidentally got other familias caught in the cross fire as well..."

Alicia, the spotter for Lefiya's support fire, started to smile.

Apparently, Orario's merchants and merchant familias had made a mysterious request for them not to kill any of the enemy soldiers. This came as a relief for Lefiya, who had never killed another person, but it required a precise control on her spells. Finn had also issued his orders with the intent to force the enemy to fall back and withdraw.

Alicia was considered a veteran even when counting the entire familia. She gently tried to soothe the younger elf, but Lefiya was her own harshest critic.

Not to torture herself, but because of her intense drive to improve.

"I dunno about the details, but I thought you were amazing! You were flinging out spells with Concurrent Casting left and right like Riveria, and the other side just kept screaming!"

"Yes, it was amazing when you blew them away. Us front-liners didn't even get to do much."

"Um, I think Mister Gareth took on a whole squad of knights or something..." Lefiya countered.

"Well, Gareth's a special case. Ahhh, to have the captain rely on you...I'm sooo jealous~."

Tiona looked up with a smile, pausing between bites of stew, jerky, and fruits to speak while Tione seemed a bit sulky as they both reassured the young girl about her contribution to the battle.

While Lefiya had been in the spotlight with her eye-catching support-fire mission, Tione and the other first-tier adventurers had gone to work elsewhere, acting as a diversion and aiming for weak points, which, in a sense, had prevented the enemy from achieving their true objectives. It was clear that Finn had put a heavy emphasis on pursuing a strategy that would prevent the situation with Rakia from getting any worse, but that was irrelevant for the Amazon who had a burning desire to be useful to the person she loved.

Lefiya laughed nervously as Tione glanced over at the boys' group, where there was one other person whom Finn valued highly—at least that's what she thought.

"Bete, let's have a meal together!"

"How about a drink?!"

"Shut it! Leave me alone! Don't crowd me, you losers! The hell's gotten into all of you?!"

"Give it up already, Bete. It was over once Loki tricked you. If ye don't want to get along with the greenhorns, then give me a hand and get me seconds."

Across from Lefiya's group, the guys had formed a lively cluster around Bete.

"Don't get cocky, old man!"

The werewolf howled as Gareth joined in on the fun.

"...They sure are in high spirits."

"To think we'd see a day when everyone wants to be around Bete..."

Anakity was exasperated while Narfi's response was filled with trepidation.

Since the recent incident, the other members of the familia had begun to idolize him. Men and women alike. Bete's bluntness had not changed, but it was having the opposite effect on people now.

Lefiya was starting to feign a laugh when a certain girl suddenly appeared, approaching Bete from behind.

"Hwa! Lena arrives on the scene! Yoo-hoo, Bete Loga!"

"Gah?! The hell are you doing here?!"

"When armies are on the march, prostitutes always follow! I tagged along with Aisha and the others when they decided to go fishing for men. All I had to do was ask, and High Novice let me right in."

"*Raul!* You dumbass! Don't just let this thing come into our camp!"

"Sorry, because of the issue with the key, I couldn't just turn her down..."

"Aisha and the others went hunting for Rakia's knights, but don't you worry—I've only got eyes for you, Bete Loga! If you're all tense from standing on the battlefield, then just let me take care of you tonight...!"

"Beat it!"

"Hng-waaah!"

Lefiya's false laughter faded as Lena cried out, her yelp tinged with an edge of pleasure. The girls lost the thread of their conversation as pandemonium unfolded on the boys' side of the camp. Shaking their heads, one after the other, they wrapped up their supper and stood to put away their dishes. The last to finish, Lefiya stood to follow the others.

...If only I had more power...

Trailing behind Tiona and the others as they chatted, Lefiya pondered the conversation they had been having earlier.

More people might have been saved if only I...Leene and the rest might still be here with us.

She understood it was a presumptuous and meaningless hypothetical, but she couldn't help herself from thinking about it. No, everyone else was surely thinking it, too.

And of course, the werewolf who couldn't stand any weakness must have felt it even more keenly than she did. They were all simply holding themselves together in order to focus on the Rakian invasion as consummate professionals.

But because Lefiya was engrossed in her hunger to improve, she never noticed.

The old Lefiya, who used to respond nervously or withered and lost her nerve at any mention of her being Riveria's successor, was gone. Her azure eyes only looked higher.

As the night deepened, she turned upward.

The starry sky and the beautiful, distant flickering of the heavens spread before her.

"…I want to be…stronger."

Softly, she whispered this to herself.

Except for the lookouts, the camp fell into slumber.

The fragrance of the grassy plains, foreign to Orario, drifted on the wind as a dim darkness enveloped everyone.

And among the sea of tents, the light of a magic-stone lantern seeped out of one of them.

"Lefiya…Are you still awake?"

Sheets rustled as her roommate, Elfie, turned to glance at her.

The sound startled Lefiya, who had been on her stomach reading a book by the light of a magic-stone lamp.

"S-sorry, Elfie, everyone. You can't sleep with the light, right?"

"Nah, I'm fine with a night-light, so it isn't a problem, but…"

The book was a treatise on magic. As Lefiya dimmed the light, Elfie and the hume bunny Rakuta made odd faces.

There was no need to obsess over developing her skills in a situation like this.

Lefiya could tell exactly what they were thinking.

They were right. Whatever she could stuff into her head right now would not allow her to gain mastery over much. It was far more important to sleep and restore as much stamina for the next day as possible.

However, Lefiya could not help but be irritated at doing nothing as time slipped away.

Loki Familia didn't have a moment to waste on venturing outside the city and getting into conflicts with other countries. They needed to develop the means to combat the groups trying to destroy the Labyrinth City or else devote their time and energy to further improving themselves. With this in mind, something resembling a compulsion had seized Lefiya.

Like I suspected, I'm bothering them, she thought.

"I'm just having a bit of trouble sleeping. I'll try getting a little fresh air," she said, picking up the thick book she had been studying. Waving at the lookouts she passed, she headed to the edge of the camp and sat on a comfortable-looking stump. It was decently far from the closest patrol, so she probably wouldn't be questioned.

Along the way, she had turned on the portable magic-stone lantern she had borrowed, and now she started reading again.

"Ah…Miss Aiz."

After a short while, a breeze blew through. As it brushed aside her long hair, Lefiya happened to glance in the direction of the wind and noticed the golden-haired, golden-eyed girl standing there.

Aiz had volunteered to keep watch because she had hardly done anything during the day. The Level-1 and Level-2 members of the familia were uncomfortable to have someone in the leadership on watch duty, but they eventually gave in to her request. Though no one had mentioned anything, Aiz probably noticed that the lower-level adventurers were getting more nervous than they were during their usual dungeon crawling. Finn had also granted his approval.

"…"

Aiz was gazing out into the plains, in the direction of the Rakian army.

But Lefiya could tell that wasn't where her eyes were focused. Since long ago, Aiz's gaze had always been fixed onto a place far off in the distance.

Lefiya was beginning to understand a bit now that she had experienced a similar feeling.

Normally, she would have gone over to greet Aiz, but tonight Lefiya only lowered her head and immersed herself once more in her attempts to absorb more knowledge.

"What are you doing, Lefiya?"

"*Gyaaa!*"

However, a voice from behind gave her a fright.

She spun around frantically and came face-to-face with Riveria, her long jade hair glimmering in the darkness. Lefiya hadn't noticed her approaching at all.

"L-Lady Riveria! Why are you here...?"

"A little while ago, Elfie came to visit me. She said you were burying yourself in books again."

"Ah..."

Beneath Riveria's stern gaze, Lefiya wilted like a child caught with her hand in the cookie jar.

"Rest. You worked harder than anyone today. If you don't recover enough Mind by tomorrow, then you will not be doing anything."

"I am truly sorry...But..."

"But what?"

"I cannot stay like this...I feel like if I don't get stronger as a mage, then I'll lose even more important things..."

"..."

"I cannot just...do nothing." Lefiya shared what was bothering her. Before Riveria could respond:

"—Ya sure are diligent, Lefiya. Even though your boobs are already this big..."

"*Kyaaa!*"

All of a sudden, someone grabbed her breasts from behind.

It was Loki. With a lewd little snort, the goddess's hands started moving. Lefiya was caught off guard, since it had been so long since this had last happened, and she didn't hold back at all as she threw Loki over her shoulder.

Sounding like a squashed frog, her muffled groan reverberated in the darkness. The various lookouts, including Aiz, started to respond to the noise but, recognizing the voice as Loki's, just continued their patrols as if nothing had happened.

"Ha-ha-ha...You've really grown, Lefiya. Escapin' my breast bind in a flash!"

"What are you doing all of a sudden?!"

"Loki, don't butt in if you intend to behave like that. It's unbearable to watch."

"I've got nothin' else to do, so I've gotta fondle me some breasts."

Lefiya and Riveria glared at Loki as she writhed on the ground where she had landed without even a hint of remorse.

Lefiya turned bright red and covered her chest as the goddess hopped back up and retrieved the book that had fallen in the shock. "Even after comin' this far, you're studying, huh? Heh-heh…Sorta reminds me of how Aizuu used to be."

"Huh?"

"I know you've been tryin' yer best until now, but this is the first time you've shown that stubborn side. That's what makes me think of Aiz all those years ago. Right, Riveria?"

"…Yes. I can see what you mean."

Surprised at the turn the conversation had taken, Lefiya froze up.

Being told that she resembled the very person she longed to emulate made her heart skip a beat.

"You wouldn't know it from seeing her now…but Aiz has really improved her manners. When she was younger, she was quite unruly. Never listening to us, always going overboard…"

Lefiya couldn't believe what she was hearing. Sure, Aiz was a bit hardheaded sometimes and occasionally made decisions without consulting others, but as a general rule, she always listened to what Riveria and Loki said. Lefiya simply could not imagine an Aiz who constantly disobeyed.

She couldn't help glancing at the golden-haired, golden-eyed swordswoman who was calmly standing in the distance.

"We were at our wits' end who knows how often. Right, Mama Riveria?"

"Quit it, Loki. Don't tease me." Riveria knit her eyebrows as Loki grinned up at her. "Anyway, she used to be very similar to how you are now, constantly rushing in and making mistakes that were unbearable to watch. Do not try to force things, Lefiya. It's fine to work hard, but don't mix that up with overwork."

Flustered for a few seconds, Lefiya made up her mind.

"U-um, then…Could you tell me a bit more about how Miss Aiz used to be?"

"Hmm?"

"I mean, if I could hear a bit more, it might be a useful lesson for me. I-it's certainly not just become I'm curious about her. I mean, o-of course I'm curious, too, but..."

Lefiya started to trip over her tongue as she tried to explain herself.

She wanted to learn about the connection between the Aiz she knew now and the Aiz of the past who she had never known. She couldn't deny that it was partly because she wanted to hear more about her idol, but she also thought there might be something useful in looking back at how the Sword Princess came to be.

Riveria looked troubled by the request, but—

"It'll be fine to tell her a bit. Just think of it as a lullaby. Will ya go to bed after ya hear it, Lefiya?"

"Y-yes!"

And that was when Loki threw her a bone.

As the goddess sat on the stump, the high elf vice captain sighed.

"Just one story. I am sure Aiz would rather not have embarrassing old stories about her spreading around. That means you cannot go sharing it, either. If that's okay with you, then I can tell you a little bit."

"P-please do!"

Lefiya leaped at the opportunity to learn more about her idol that had just fallen into her lap.

Glancing over at where Aiz was standing watch, Riveria said, "Let's go elsewhere so she doesn't overhear us and try to cut us to pieces."

Lefiya could not tell how serious she was as she started to move. The young elf followed along with Loki to the second-in-command's personal tent.

Riveria lit a lamp, glancing at Loki in annoyance as the goddess made herself at home.

"It was nine years ago when we first met...A lot of things happened leading up to that winter day when Aiz was placed in our care."

THE YOUNG

GIRL'S

BEGINNINGS

Гэта казка іншага сям.

Пачатак дзяўчыны

"Are you sure about this?" the goddess asked.

She stood facing a small back.

The skin was unbelievably smooth and pale.

Untouched by violence, as if antithetical to the very idea of it.

"If I do this, there's no goin' back, ya know?"

The goddess checked one more time as she gave her final warning. Her vermilion hair wavered. Blood seeped from the cut on her finger.

"That's part of becomin' a god's follower."

The little girl had only one response.

"Hurry and do it."

Her voice did not waver in the slightest; her determination was sharp like steel.

An unwavering resolution. Her golden eyes, fixed straight ahead, were the same. In them was a cold gaze like an unsheathed blade that would cut through any- and everything. It was too sharp for a child not yet even ten to wield. The goddess could sense only danger in the girl's future from it.

The goddess looked down and softly put her finger on the girl's back.

Her flowing blood slowly drew out the letters of the gods.

The line of characters was like an inscription, vermilion hiero-glyphs reminiscent of a sunset.

Once the goddess's and girl's true names were inscribed, the Blessing announced to the world that another god's follower had been born.

"Welcome to *Loki Familia*. Now yer one of my followers."

"Rose."

The bored werewolf receptionist waiting at the counter looked up when she heard her name.

Before her eyes was a high elf who possessed peerless beauty.

Rose had been chosen by the Guild in part for her good looks, but she could not hold a candle to the high elf. It was a bit of a well-known story around the Labyrinth City that this unrivaled high elf had even inspired the jealousy of a goddess, setting off a full-blown incident. The jade hair gathered around her collar was jewellike, befitting the dignified aura of a high-level magic user.

However, the young receptionist was neither entranced nor jealous of those looks. She did not even fix her bored slouch as she responded—seeming more annoyed by the hassle than displeased.

"Welcome, *Loki Familia* Vice Captain Riveria Ljos Alf. What brings you here today?"

"You can stop with the formal greetings, Rose. You're not even acting like you mean it."

"It says in the manual that we're supposed to do that for the major familias, so I can't help it, you know? If we don't do what we're supposed to, we get a pay cut."

Riveria furrowed her brows in a dignified way, to which the werewolf responded while twirling her red hair with one hand.

They were in Guild Headquarters, located in the city's northwest district. This organization was the main administrative force in Orario, which had neither king nor feudal lord. Whether past, present, or future, it served as the Labyrinth City's core.

"Five years ago, when I first met you behind the counter, you were so innocent. You've really changed. I think you were fourteen then? That willfulness hasn't gone anywhere, though."

"That was right after I started the job. Could you please not bring up things from forever ago?"

"For an elf like me, it's not all that different from something that happened only a month ago."

The sun shone into the lobby as adventurers and workers bustled around. Rose sullenly crossed her arms. She was wearing a black uniform provided by the Guild and, at the moment, emphasizing the one area where she could win against Riveria. She responded with an overfamiliar tone of voice.

"Well? I'm sure you didn't come to shoot the breeze. If this is gonna be a pain, I'd rather you hurry up and get it over with. They get fussy over every little thing when we deal with you guys or *Freya Familia.*"

As if confirming what she said, all the Guild staff behind the counter glanced over at the two of them.

Silenced for a moment, Riveria nodded and responded.

"Yes…Registering an adventurer. I'd like you to process someone."

Rose looked confused.

"Registering an adventurer…And where is said new adventurer? I can't register someone if they aren't here themselves."

"She's here."

"Huh?"

"The new adventurer is here."

Following Riveria's gaze downward, Rose leaned over the counter.

Like she said, there was indeed a person standing there. A young human, still so small that the counter was enough to hide her. A golden-haired, golden-eyed young girl wearing plain clothes.

Rose's eyes widened. Despite the girl's age, her beauty rivaled Riveria's. Her golden eyes were particularly striking; in them dwelled a strong, determined light that was entirely at odds with the rest of her appearance. Her gaze contained a steely resolve unbefitting a child.

"I would like to register this girl as an adventurer."

"…All right, all right. I'll take care of it."

Rose bluntly accepted the request.

Assuming a professional attitude, she suppressed a reproachful glare and swallowed what she really wanted to say as she started the registration process.

"Can you write?"

"…"

The little girl nodded in response to Riveria's question.

Standing on a stool made for prum adventurers, she grabbed the quill pen offered to her and started to write on the provided parchment.

"…Wait, those are hieroglyphs? Use Koine."

"?!"

Rose was shocked as Riveria helped the girl fill out the registration sheet's required sections.

Name...Aiz Wallenstein. Age seven, eh? And absolutely nothing else...

Place of birth was blank, background was blank, everything else was blank, blank, blank...A void that told nothing. Other than her age, no information was listed at all.

Rose frowned but didn't say anything.

This was Orario. Outlaws looking to get rich quick and people with guilty consciences came here all the time. And the Guild welcomed anyone who could take on the Dungeon. If they investigated everyone who didn't reveal their past or career, it would never end.

Other than special cases like spies or informants working for other countries or cities, anybody could become an adventurer. That was the rule here. Rose accepted the parchment and approved it, like always.

"As for an adviser...Well, you guys won't need that. A big familia like yours doesn't need any support from us."

"Yes, we'll take care of her instruction ourselves."

The Guild had instituted a system of advisers, mainly to assist newly established familias and novice adventurers, but it was unnecessary for one of the largest and most famous groups in Orario.

At that, Aiz Wallenstein looked up at the high elf.

"Is it...over?"

"...Yes. The registration is done."

"Then I'm going."

Despite just meeting her, Rose could tell from that curt exchange that the little girl was heading for the Dungeon.

The sharp-eyed girl jumped off the stool, about to dash off. But before she could leave, Riveria grabbed her by the collar of her shirt.

"Wait, you fool. Do you really intend to go straight to the Dungeon?"

The girl coughed cutely before glaring like she was about to get revenge for her parents. Not that the expression could possibly faze a first-tier adventurer.

"Going into the Dungeon without any preparation is suicide. What exactly were you planning to do without a weapon, at least?"

"Tch…"

"The first step is obtaining equipment. You need weapons and armor."

Riveria won the argument with sound reasoning. Blushing slightly in embarrassment, Aiz glared at her before giving in reluctantly.

"…Want to use the Guild's stock?"

Watching the exchange from the sidelines, Rose cut in.

"Yes, please. Those will be perfect for a novice who doesn't know anything."

"I never thought I'd see the day I'd be offering beginner's adventurer equipment to *Loki Familia*. All right, dear, follow this clerk to get your measurements taken."

She called over one of the women behind the counter to lead Aiz aside. The human worker held out her hand, but the girl refused to take it, simply following behind silently like a doll.

"Someone who can write *hieroglyphs*. Did you abduct her from some kingdom? Or one of the professors in the Education District?"

"Do not pry. That's all I can say."

"Hmm…Well, whatever. Though we'd rather you do something about the Evils than mess around with new adventurers."

"That's a bit of a sore spot."

The two spoke without looking at each other, focused only on the unsmiling little girl who was having her measurements taken.

"So the city's biggest faction is planning to arm a small child with a sword, then send her to die in the Dungeon?"

"…"

"You're that desperate to expand your faction's influence? If so, I gravely misjudged you."

"…"

"Even if she wanted it herself, isn't it the job of the adults in the room to stop her?"

"…"

Once they were alone, Rose unleashed all the opinions she had been holding back. They were her true feelings, her criticisms as a Guild employee who had seen too many adventurers rush to their deaths.

Riveria did not respond. Glancing over, Rose saw that the high elf was trying her best not to show any emotion, so she ended her tirade.

Rose had only just met the girl, after all.

To her eyes, it looked like Riveria was also trying to figure out how to cross the moat that the little girl had dug around herself.

"That one's headed for an early grave."

She ended with her appraisal as a member of the Guild.

"A fast life doesn't begin to describe it. I've met a lot of adventurers, but that's the first time I've seen eyes like that. The moment you look away, she's gonna get herself killed."

Riveria had a clear answer to Rose's warning.

"I won't allow it," she declared. "That's why we are here."

This air is familiar. When I was younger, I stumbled into here.

The moment Aiz stepped in, she remembered that sensation.

As she felt the vaguely cool air on her skin, her eyes took in her surroundings.

Despite being underground, phosphorescence lit the area. The dim blue walls and ceiling indicated that this was the entrance of the labyrinth.

This was the first floor of the Dungeon, in the Upper Levels.

Passing through the spiral staircase to the big pit below Babel and beyond the wide Beginning Road, Aiz and Riveria arrived at a certain corner of the labyrinth. There was a single path to follow, with no forks in the road. However, Aiz seemed agitated as she stood out front. Excessively so, as if she was tackling the most stressful thing in the world. Her sharp gaze searched for any hint of monsters.

"Quit tensing up so much. You are breathing too shallowly. What are you going to do later if something as minor as this wrecks your nerves?"

Despite being only a few steps behind her, Aiz didn't hear Riveria's words. The young girl tightened her grip on the sword in her hands. She had a Guild-provided straight sword, quaintly named Little Blade. It was a weapon generally used by prums, but it was perfect for Aiz, who was not even 120 celch tall. Her armor had also been provided by the Guild, something called Little Leather also intended for use by prums.

Her leather boots creaking, Aiz proceeded step by step into the Dungeon. She noticed that her field of vision was narrowing. When it became too hard to breathe, she finally realized that she had been hyperventilating. Her body had become so tense, she could barely move at all.

Become strong.

She had no idea whether she was feeling nervousness, exultation, or something else altogether.

I have to become strong.

But Aiz realized that she was, at this moment, standing at the starting line.

For my wish, no matter what.

It announced the end of her life as a naive little girl. There was no one who would protect her anymore. Or at least that was what she believed.

Having taken up such a scary weapon and accepted its profound weight, she had no choice but to wield it.

That's why I'll…fight monsters.

Aiz wished for power.

She had insisted that she had to become strong.

And in response, they had—*Loki Familia* had met her demand.

It's fine as long as I can go to the Dungeon.

If she received a Blessing, roamed the Dungeon, and defeated monsters, she would obtain the power she was looking for. That was what they had said.

Riveria watched in silence with an inscrutable expression as the girl crossed her starting line.

The moment Aiz had been so desperately waiting for finally came.

"Graaa..."

"!"

Short limbs and a chubby torso. Greenish skin. A goblin. One of the monsters native to the first floor and a common low-level creature for adventurers to face first.

Standing before her on the path, the goblin bared its small fangs and growled. Aiz's heart skipped a beat. Her back grew hot where the Blessing had been inscribed, as if it contained a black flame.

"Don't rush in thoughtlessly. Don't think about killing it in one blow, either. Just—"

Riveria's advice was ignored before she even had a chance to finish. Aiz dashed forward without listening to her instructions at all.

"Tch! Fool!"

The elf's rebuke fell on deaf ears as the young girl charged with her sword held high.

Despite yelling at her, Riveria made no move to help. She had already determined that even if the goblin landed a counterattack on the young girl, it would not be able to inflict a lethal wound. Also, it was important to learn from mistakes. That was what she thought.

Then something unexpected happened.

Golden hair fluttered.

A slash came down with all her weight behind it.

The monster was *in pieces*.

"___"

"Gyaaaaaaa?!!!"

Flesh scattered, blood sprayed, and the creature raised a dying cry. Its limbs ripped apart, the ugly monster turned into an even uglier lump of meat. It had taken only an instant for a slash from Little Blade to fell the monster.

Riveria was at a loss. It looked more like the monster had been hit with a sledgehammer than with a blade.

One strike.

The goblin was dead from a single strike.

The first strike of a Level-1 adventurer who had just obtained her Status should not be that strong.

It was an unbelievable result—overkill.

This marked the very first battle of the adventurer known as Aiz Wallenstein, as well as her first victory.

"This…"

Aiz stood up straight, her upper body covered in gore from the clumsy slash. Her lips trembled as she whispered subconsciously.

"…This…is the first…"

The inaugural kill.

Her first step past the starting line.

However, no emotions swelled in her chest. There was no sense of achievement, no excitement, nothing. Covered in blood, she seemed disinterested as she surveyed the results of the fight.

This was only the first stop along the way. The road to reach the strength she desired was so long that such a small step mattered very little in comparison to the goal in the distance.

That was why Aiz ran.

She screamed to fan the flames of her fighting spirit, her chest quivering.

Drawn by the girl's cry and the scent of their kin's blood, a mob of monsters gathered ahead on the path.

Riveria came to her senses and tried to keep Aiz in check, but the young girl shook her off and headed deeper, slicing into the pack of howling monsters.

The sword created a symphony of dull thuds, leaving countless wounds in its wake.

Along with monstrous screams.

"This can't be…It's impossible."

That was all Riveria could do to put into words the scene that unfolded before her.

"*Goghaaa!*"

"——*AAA?!*"

Whenever the girl unleashed a strike with all her strength, any monsters standing before her were blown to bits.

Just like the first goblin, hunks of their flesh scattered.

"Uuuuaaaahhhh!!"

To Riveria, it was plain brute force. The girl put her weight behind the prum-size sword and leaned into every attack right as she started to fall. However, the force contained in that blow was more than enough to slay a goblin or a kobold. Their menacing growls quickly changed to yelps of fear. Because of her strength attribute, the sword itself was already wearing down.

It was a bizarre sight—monsters' arms and legs strewn about while the wall was splattered with fresh blood everywhere. A normal person would never associate the carnage with this girl who couldn't properly wield a sword and had no idea how to fight. As Aiz continued to snarl and charge at the monsters, Riveria felt a chill.

"Ha!!"

"Gegee?!"

Riveria shuddered as Aiz finished off the last remaining monster. Gritting her teeth with all her might, the girl fully committed to a slash that struck the kobold in its torso. The monster's body crumbled along with its magic stone, turning to ash.

"Haaa-haaa-haaa..."

The only sound left was the girl's ragged breath echoing in the Dungeon.

"...Aiz, that'll be all for today. We're going back."

Riveria could tell that Aiz's condition was getting dangerous and decided it was time to return.

"I can still...keep going..."

Aiz's desire to fight was still high, and she backed away when the elf held out her hand.

Then something suddenly fell out of Aiz's mouth with a *plop*.

"Ah..."

"...?"

The girl seemed shocked as she realized what had happened. Riveria dubiously leaned over and picked up the object that had fallen from Aiz's mouth.

"This is..."

The shining white thing lying in Riveria's open palm was not a magic stone or anything of the sort, nor was it a drop item—it was a baby tooth.

"Ga-ha-ha-haaa!"

Loki burst into laughter as she examined the cute little baby tooth.

"Usin' so much strength that ya lose a tooth?! That's rich! But yeah, yeah, makes sense. Aizuu's just a sweet li'l seven-year-old girl, after all!"

"But to grit your teeth so hard while you're fighting…"

Finn smiled with chagrin from behind his desk as Loki rudely kicked her feet up on it, holding her stomach after too much laughing.

They were in the office of *Loki Familia*'s home. Loki, Finn, and Gareth were present, along with Aiz and Riveria, who had just returned from the Dungeon. They had come to report on Aiz's debut after she registered at the Guild.

Aiz was blushing as she avoided making eye contact.

"Hey, Aizuu! Smile and say 'cheese'! I wanna see that cute little gap-toothed smile of yours!"

"Don't wanna."

Aiz turned away and headed for the door as Loki approached with a lecherous grin.

"I'm leaving."

"—Not a chance! Gareth!"

All of a sudden, the goddess snapped her fingers. Sighing, the dwarf closed in and lifted Aiz like a feather.

"Gh—?! L-let me go!"

"Bwa-ha-ha-ha! I'm the goddess here!"

Hoisted by her arms, Aiz swung her legs helplessly as Loki immediately started her attack. Narrowly avoiding any perverted locations in a calculated manner, she began to tickle Aiz.

"~~~~~—Ngh?!"

"Come on now—open yer mouth for me!"

The little girl's eyes went wide as her stomach was assaulted by two hands' worth of fingers. Resistance was futile, and in seconds she burst out in exclamation.

"Sto—Gya-haaa! Stop it! Ah-ah-ha-ha-ha!!"

Riveria put her hand on her cheek and turned away while Finn's familiar exasperation appeared on his face. Aiz blushed bright red, tears in her eyes as her mouth opened wide.

Loki peered in and saw the gap where the upper molar next to her canine had fallen out, leaving her gums visible.

"Ah-ha-ha! Sooo cute! I'll hold on to that memory forever! I'm gonna cherish this tooth!"

After her guffaws died down, Loki wrapped the tooth in a scarf like she was preparing it for the afterlife.

Soon they settled down.

Containing her involuntary laughter, Aiz gradually stood up, her golden eyes blazing. She closed in on Loki with tremendous speed and lashed out with a leg sweep.

"Hmph!"

"Gugyaaaaaaaaaaaaaaaaaaaaaaaaaaaaaaaaaaaaaaaaaaaaaaaaaaaaaaa?!"

Now that she had received a Blessing, the young child's low kick was backed by enhanced strength that could slay even monsters, and that attack scored a clean hit on Loki's shin. The goddess rolled around while cradling her leg as Riveria and the others tried to suppress the headaches they felt coming on. Furious enough that even her ears seemed red, Aiz didn't give Loki so much as a second glance when she finally left the room.

The goddess's coarse wails echoed around for a little while longer.

"...So how was it, Riveria? How did she seem?"

Judging that the young girl was now far enough away, Loki stood up as if she had been faking all along. Her demeanor was dead serious, nothing like her ridiculous performance earlier.

Meeting her gaze, Riveria shared her impressions of the girl.

"For the most part, it went as expected. No thought at all about the danger to herself. Because of her goal, she is too obsessed with power."

"'I want power,' huh? It's not my place to talk about other people's wishes, but that girl's desire is a bit too direct. It's dangerous. And it's painful to watch."

Finn smiled sadly as he leaned back in his chair. Then, as if just realizing something, he soon raised a question.

"Good job getting her out of the Dungeon, Riveria. Seems like she would have kept fighting until she collapsed. Was that little baby tooth how you did it?"

"No. Before she had a chance to collapse, her weapon gave out. That was when she started listening again."

"What's that? Even if it was one of the Guild's stock weapons, it shouldn't be falling apart from spending half a day with a greenhorn…"

Riveria drew the shortsword at her waist, the Little Blade she had taken from Aiz, then handed it to Gareth. Sliding it out of the scabbard, he noticed the blade clearly had significant chunks missing. The dwarf could not contain his surprise as he examined the weapon in his hand.

"She killed monsters with one blow…*literally blowing them to pieces*. That is not a feat that should be possible for a Level-One adventurer."

"Do you think…it was that Skill?" Loki raised her eyebrow a bit.

"Anything else would be unthinkable." Riveria confirmed her suspicions. "That is an amazing Skill…but it's also the chain dragging her closer to death."

What had happened in the Dungeon replayed itself in Riveria's mind. Defeating too many monsters summoned more enemies, leading to a dangerous predicament. Then there was also Aiz's lack of concern for her wounds.

Looking into the elf's jade eyes, the others sighed with a tinge of anxiety.

"Guess we can't be tellin' her about that magic like this…"

"Yes. If we provided her a powerful weapon, it'd only be putting her in even more danger. She isn't ready yet."

Looking down, Gareth responded as if he saw something in the broken sword.

Loki had not told the girl about the magic ability that had appeared on her Status. It was obvious that the moment she learned about that colossal power, she would force herself to keep fighting without end.

"First, we need a way to control that Skill…If we can't instill a mind capable of controlling those emotions, this is hopeless. What she needs now isn't physical conditioning. It's mental training."

Finn, Gareth, and Loki all nodded in agreement with Riveria's conclusion.

"Yeah, let's get to it…So we wanna teach her how to think like an adventurer—or more like how to fight and just, like, general knowledge, yeah? Plus an education on how to act like an upstandin' person. Someone's gotta teach her."

"Teach? But who…"

"…"

"…"

"…"

Silence fell in the room as everyone focused on Riveria.

Sensing their silent gazes, the mage looked up, flustered.

"Wait a minute…Me?"

"Unfortunately, the captain can't really focus on a single member. And I have to deal with the Evils, too. Of course, I'll make time to check in on how it's going."

"Is my job description not vice captain?! What about Gareth?!"

"I got a slew of annoying missions still. And I ain't sure how to put it nicely, but I dunno the first thing about how to handle a lass that age. It'd probably be easier for Aiz to have a woman watching over her, right?"

"That's a convenient excuse!"

"And besides, Riveria, you were the one who volunteered to watch over Aizuu today. Doesn't she bring out your motherly instinct?"

Finn and Gareth shrugged helplessly while Loki smiled provocatively.

"Don't make assumptions, Loki!"

"It's a perfect opportunity. Riveria's gonna be a mama!"

"I'm unmarried and you know it!"

"I know, I know. High elves can hide their age, but ya should give it a try before yer too old to get married."

"Hmph!"

"*Iggyaaa?!*"

She swung her staff much more sharply than Aiz's kick, hitting Loki in the shin again and provoking another scream. Red with fury, Riveria glared down at the goddess rolling around the floor. Finn and Gareth awkwardly laughed while watching the two's antics.

"Jokes aside, I actually do think you are the right person for the job, Riveria."

"Finn…You are expecting too much from me. Taking care of a girl, from a different race no less. I can't…"

"Then let's put it this way. It's the captain's order."

Finn's eyes contained a playful glint as he announced his decision.

"Aiz is a member of our familia now. Welcoming her in is our job as adults. We have to receive her with an affection that would match her real family's."

"…"

"Of course I think it'll be rough, but we'll help out, too. I've no intention of foisting it all on you, after all."

"That's what being friends is about, right?"

Finn smiled gently and Gareth grinned a hearty grin.

And finally, a teary-eyed Loki stood up, massaging her leg.

"I also think it's important for you personally, Riveria. From now on, there'll be more little ones joinin' our familia, so it's important for them to know a mama's touch."

Riveria's expression was incredibly severe, but she finally gave in. Apparently resigned to her fate, she blushed, looked away, and offered one final protest.

"Who are you calling mama…?"

Thunk!

Several large books landed atop the desk.

"...What is this?"

Aiz suspiciously eyed the mountain of books piled in front of her.

The day after her first trip into the Dungeon, she had been practically dragged to Riveria's room after she finished breakfast.

Even for someone like Aiz, who had held little interest in other races at the time, she could tell the room belonged to an elf. There were a lot of wooden things. Something about the ceiling was different. Magic-stone lamps resembling flowers and fruits had been placed next to the simple bed and atop the desk that was covered by a stack of parchments—probably familia-related documents.

Her silver staff leaned against a shelf decorated with a vase containing an arrangement of pure-white flowers. Alongside it was a large, clear bottle with a young budding tree growing inside. Probably both from her elf village. Magic potions and beautiful gems—spare magic jewels—were neatly lined up on other shelves. By and large, the documents and things occupying the shelves were an expression of the room's occupant.

Aiz sat in a chair in the middle of the large room, uneasy at all the different things around her as she looked up at Riveria.

"Starting today, we're going to be working on your fundamentals. In short, studying."

"...Studying...?"

"Yes. About the Dungeon, obviously, but also about skills and magic and such. I'll be teaching you the mind-set of an adventurer."

"...I don't need that. Just let me fight."

"Fool. Do you really think you can become stronger without even knowing what it means to fight? If you desire strength, then you must first comprehend the things you don't yet know and strive to rectify that lack of knowledge."

Riveria casually shot down Aiz, ignoring her glowering look.

Aiz had trouble dealing with the high elf. Having just joined, she still was not really used to anyone in *Loki Familia* and felt some distance between her and them, but spending time with this woman was particularly bad.

They had only just met, and she was so overbearing and nagging. Aiz had known a female elf like that before, but this Riveria person was far more overbearing than she had ever been. It brought back memories long buried from her youth—though it was only two or three years past—that elf scolding her until she cried countless times. She could not hide her immense discontent.

"Ah-ha-ha! Ya hate studyin', huh, Aizuu?"

Loki had invited herself in along with Aiz. She smiled as she constructed a house of cards on the other end of the desk. She had come to see how Riveria was faring on the first day of her teaching assignment, but there was no way Aiz knew that.

Ugh. She gulped.

Loki had hit the mark, but the girl sullenly refused to answer.

"Aiz, what you need is the 'great tree's spirit' that is essential for us mages. You need to develop a state of mind that will not be swayed by anything. If you continue to fight by relying on your Skill like you did yesterday, you will inevitably self-destruct."

Riveria explained the situation in a clear voice without any hesitation or mumbling.

However, as far as Aiz was concerned, the elf's bell-like explanation might as well have been gibberish.

What are you saying?

What are you even talking about?

It doesn't make any sense at all.

Wasn't I clear that I don't wanna study? Just let me get a new weapon and fight. Isn't that obviously the fastest way to get stronger? Why is this elf so full of herself?

She kept trying to make Aiz do things she did not want to do, annoying and angering the girl. That frustration kept building, summoning more anger until she couldn't totally hold it in anymore. Trembling slightly, she hung her head.

"Why don't ya just give it a chance, Aizuu? Aren't ya happy to have such a beauty around all the time as a mentor? Hee-hee-hee, the cute little girl and her gorgeous governess...That's a great pairing. Hey, Riveria, could ya put on a pair of glasses for me?"

"What the hell are you talking about?"

While Loki and Riveria kept talking, Aiz's irritation finally hit her limit. A strained whisper escaped her.

"—Was way prettier."

Looking up at Riveria and Loki, Aiz's face was scrunched into a furious glare.

"Old hag!"

She screamed at Riveria.

" .... "

"Eeep!"

Loki genuinely gasped when she saw the high elf's facial expression freeze over in an instant.

Riveria's eyes narrowed. Not noticing the sudden change, Aiz stared at her defiantly, and then, before her eyes could even catch what was happening, the elf's fist swung down.

The next instant—*bonk!*

"?!!!!"

It was an iron fist.

Lightning had landed on the back of Aiz's head. Between the pain and the shock, she could not respond. The force behind it was so great that she could even feel it in her tailbone sitting in the chair.

The world was spinning. Or at least it felt like it was.

"It seems you need to learn proper respect for your elders first."

Holding the top of her head with both hands to soothe the ache, Aiz quivered at the curt tone of the elf beside her. Even Loki was afraid, swallowing her usual jokes. Nervously looking up, Aiz actually shuddered when she saw the high elf glaring daggers at her.

"Let me be clear. I *will* punish excessively impertinent comments."

As the high elf stared down at her with a frozen expression and cold eyes, Aiz felt an uncontrollable terror for the first time. At the same moment, she also realized the difference in their strength.

If I'm a goblin like one of the dozens I killed yesterday, then she's one of the "crazy strong" Monster Rexes Father and everyone else talked about...!

"We're starting. Pick up the pen. Note down everything I'm about to tell you, and etch it into your brain."

"...?!"

Loki put a hand to her face and muttered, "She's done it now," as Aiz, trembling in terror, finally began obeying the high elf.

The next day arrived.

On the second day of studies, Aiz quickly escaped from Riveria's lectures.

"Where are you, Aiz?! Come back here!"

Aiz stealthily kept her distance, hiding from the terrifying high elf, whose voice was audible even one tower over in the manor. Fortunately, she didn't run into anyone else in the hallways or on the stairs, so no one could give away her hiding spot.

The Twilight Manor was almost entirely empty. She did not know the specifics, but apparently Orario's public order was in disarray at the moment, and practically every member of the familia was running around responding to various quests and mandatory missions handed down from above.

Aiz had already decided that Riveria was the queen of terror.

I really don't get that elf at all. Aiz was admittedly not that great at studying to begin with, but she could not help feeling that the standards she was imposing were insane. *What's with all those books?! There's no way I can remember so much stuff!* She still had a headache because of the intense study session the day before.

It had been enough that even the usually easygoing Loki awkwardly tried to persuade Riveria to rein it in a bit. "Come on, Riveria—it's just the first day, after all, so go a little easier on her..."

I don't wanna study anymore...I hate studying...

Crawling around between the towers on all fours, Aiz unleashed all her frustrations in her mind. She had already developed a severe allergy to giant tomes. Her face was scrunched up like she had just eaten her most hated food, and she trembled as the image of that devil teacher flashed across her mind.

There isn't even any point in studying. I don't have the time to waste on something like that...

As her frustrations boiled over, she felt an impatience to match her discontent.

There were other things she needed to be doing. What she wanted was something else.

The strength to realize her wish. Weapons that could kill monsters. What Aiz wanted could be achieved only on the battlefield.

Sneaking into a deserted archive, Aiz sat down in a small opening at the corner of the room between bookshelves, burying her head in her knees.

I have to...get stronger...

Feeling an uncontrollable desire weighing on her little chest, Aiz squeezed her eyes shut.

"...?"

Suddenly, Aiz felt something was off.

Going to the Dungeon and fighting monsters had given her the seeds of an adventurer's sense, though imperfect, and it alerted her to the change in the situation. Noticing a presence, she looked up.

"Hey."

In front of her, a prum man smiled at her.

"*Guh?!*"

"Uh-oh. You all right there?"

Taken aback, she had tried to retreat and hit her head on the wall.

While stars were bursting before her eyes, he squatted down, looking concerned about her.

How did he know I was here? No, where did he even come from? I didn't notice him approaching at all.

Aiz looked shocked as the prum, Finn, still smiling, tilted his head.

"Why...? This is...?"

"Mm, because you were desperate to get away from Riveria, it was easy for someone who was in a different location to sneak up on you."

Just as Aiz started to wonder if he had told on her to Riveria, he cheerfully added, "I haven't told Riveria," as if he had read her mind.

"She can be a bit too serious about her jobs, so I figured you'd eventually try to escape...I didn't think you'd already be there by the second day, though."

Aiz felt uncomfortably trapped as a strained smile drifted across Finn's face.

She did not really understand the prum they called Finn yet.

She had been told he was head of their group, but she didn't really get that sort of impression from him. It seemed he always had that gentle smile on his face. She couldn't explain it, but she had the feeling that he was easier to deal with than Riveria.

Since he was about the same height as her, he met her eye to eye.

"Was Riveria's lecture that rough? Do you hate it already?"

He looked like a boy at first glance, but his appearance was at odds with his mature voice, which left Aiz furrowing her brows. He was naturally getting involved in this as part of his role as the familia's captain.

"I have to become stronger. Let me fight! I don't have time to waste studying!"

All the frustrations and emotions that Aiz had been holding in finally came rushing out.

"Studying is pointless!"

Her voice reverberated in the archive.

Having listened to her complaints in silence, Finn suddenly stood up.

"*Hmph.* Then shall we head outside?"

"Eh?"

"You want to fight, right? Then I'll be your opponent."

He smiled that same gentle smile as Aiz reacted with confusion.

"How about some combat studies?"

Finn brought her to the manor's central yard, surrounded by various towers.

Because it was visible from any of the towers, she wondered for a second whether he was simply trying to let Riveria find her, but he said, "If Riveria shows up, I'll explain to her. I promise."

What they were doing now was a mock battle. She was supposed to fight Finn as if he was an enemy.

Aiz held a training shortsword. The edge was intentionally dull, but it was still made of metal and had a fair amount of heft as a blunt weapon. A hit from that would still be plenty painful.

On the other side, Finn was holding a broom with the brush removed—a wooden pole.

Finn took a couple of practice swings to check how it felt before turning to face Aiz.

"Um..."

"Hmm? What's up?"

"Is that...okay?"

"Ah, my weapon? Don't worry about it—it'd just be a waste."

She froze a bit as the prum casually responded with a smile.

Just like her future self, she was a tomboy who hated to lose.

"All right, let's do it. Come at me however you like."

She didn't need to be told twice.

Readying her sword, she shifted into a battle stance, measured her timing, and rushed at him.

"Charging in from the front. Hmm, easy to read."

"?!"

Finn disappeared before her eyes, and she stumbled as her slash missed its mark. She swiveled around wildly, but her opponent was just standing behind her without a care in the world, that same smile still pasted across his face.

Enraged, Aiz flew in again with her sword.

"Your resolve is respectable, and your swings have a nice sharp edge to them. There's the glimmer of something there."

"Guh!"

"But unfortunately, that's not enough in a fight."

Finn kept chatting as he continued to dodge Aiz's wild slashes without breaking a sweat.

Even if she was only seven years old, she had still received a Status, so the attacks she dealt out had force and speed behind them. However, what had worked on the monsters she fought before was entirely useless against this adventurer. Finn was not doing anything particularly special, either. He did not counterattack and simply choose to nimbly evade her. He wasn't even moving especially quickly or working in any impressive parries.

He was just casually facing Aiz and circling around her.

"—...?!"

I can't hit him. I can't hit him at all. Not even a scratch.

Before she realized it, Aiz was gritting her teeth and putting her whole body into swinging the sword.

"That Skill isn't going to work on me."

But Finn dodged even that attack without batting an eye.

Despite trying a violent blow using her whole body, the only sound that rang out was the *whoosh* of a big whiff. Aiz tried it again as beads of sweat rolled down her cheek and her breathing became ragged.

Around the fifth time he dodged her attack, he tripped her up as she passed him, sending her tumbling down onto the grass.

"You done?"

"*Kuh...Waaaa!!*"

Standing up, Aiz screamed in a blind fury as she swung her sword around.

She did not notice the person watching them fight as she tried to cut Finn countless times—and went rolling across the ground just as many times.

Finally, Finn started to counterattack. Using the tip of the wooden pole, he poked her waist or her arm, as if pointing out her mistakes.

He did not put much strength into the blows, but it was enough to knock Aiz onto her butt.

"Yep. *Weak*."

"*Grrr—?!*"

Then he hit Aiz once with a stronger attack.

Blown back, she collapsed faceup on the grass. The training sword thudded against the ground beside her. Finally unable to move, Aiz looked up at the blue sky in disbelief.

The prum walked over to her, his golden hair swaying in the wind as he calmly looked down at her.

"Your style of fighting relies on the strength of your Status...of your Skill. When we remove that from the equation, this is what happens."

"...!"

Aiz's cheeks turned a bright red, a mixture of her frustration from the fight and her personal embarrassment. Finn continued as she dragged herself up to a sitting position.

"Us first-tier adventurers often say that many adventurers are controlled by their Status."

"Huh...?"

"Lots of people rely too much on their Blessing. That is not the same thing as your ability and techniques."

Aiz's ears stung, recognizing the implied *just like you* in his tone.

"What you lack are techniques and strategy. And, more than anything else, knowledge."

"!"

"Not only do you not know how to approach an enemy—you don't even understand the idiosyncrasies of your own weapon. You are truly just a child. Even if you go to the Dungeon, as you are now, you'll only end up getting yourself killed. I guarantee it."

Finn smiled softly as Aiz's golden eyes went wide.

"Aiz, we never started out strong. We grew from lots of training on top of a ton of adventuring and, yes, studying, too—Isn't that right, Riveria?"

"...Yes."

Aiz gasped and swung around. Riveria was standing at the entrance connecting the courtyard to the tower. She had been watching their mock battle the whole time. Stepping down onto the grass, she approached them.

"There was so much I had to learn. And just as much I had to experience and practice. When I encountered things I didn't know in the world, I endeavored to learn everything I could..."

"..."

"In order to achieve my desire."

Hesitating for a second, Riveria offered her hand. Aiz was taken aback, looking between the elf's hand and her face. She wavered for a moment, then finally reached out.

The slightly cool hand helped her stand up.

"Aiz, your wish...It's a lot more difficult than our desires and goals. If you want to achieve it, then you're going to have to survive the things we went through and struggle even more than we did. Do you understand that?"

Hanging her head at Finn's question, Aiz slowly nodded.

After going through the mock battle, she had become painfully aware of their difference in ability and could finally begin to understand the heavy implication behind his words.

Just how rash and reckless she was being. How narrow her field of view had become.

She was beginning to see how big the world really was.

She finally understood it.

"I can't give you permission to explore the Dungeon for a while, but if Gareth or I have time, we'll do some physical training with you, like today."

"!"

"Just like you wanted, we'll teach you how to fight. So keep at it during Riveria's lectures. I want you to strengthen your mind and your body."

After smiling at Aiz, Finn turned to Riveria.

"So, Riveria. As an elder deserving of respect, do you have anything to say?"

"..."

As if she had been thinking about it all along, Riveria fell silent for a moment and then spoke directly to Aiz.

"Aiz...I was too intense before. I handled myself poorly. I am sorry."

Aiz was visibly shocked at her apology. The woman's gaze and words conveyed a deep regret and an unfamiliar but sincere parental concern.

Just a little—really just a tiny bit—Aiz's chest tightened. It was all she could do to nod.

"Me too...I'm sorry."

For some reason, she could not bring herself to look up, so she stared down at the grass as she spoke.

"Please...help me study."

She bowed her head.

Riveria's expression showed her surprise for a moment before changing to a smile.

"Yes. I'll try my best."

It was early morning, before the sun had begun to rise.

Aiz made her way down to the courtyard holding a sword. Cloaked in the early dawn, the manor was silent. The cool air caressed her skin as she gazed up at the dark sky. Aiz felt like she understood a little bit of the secret behind the strength that Riveria and the others possessed.

They had gradually built it up. It was the product of an actual mountain of experience.

And it wasn't just them.

Surely her father and the other brave people with him had done the same.

"..."

Embracing the loneliness in her heart, she steeled herself and drew the sword that Finn had given her.

"Simply, soundly, and steadily build your strength."

When Riveria had told her that, Aiz made up her mind. In order to fulfill her wish, she would put in more work than they ever had. She would be more resolute than they were.

With a strong determination in her chest, she began to swing her sword by herself.

Her unending effort would persist without interruption into the distant future.

A
BRIEF
CALM

Гэта казка іншага сям

◆

Мімалётнае статычныя скрытыя

"We're returning to the city. Start getting ready."

This was the fifth day since the battle had begun.

The conflict with Rakia was still ongoing when Finn gave that order.

"It seems like Rakia just wants to drag out this war for some reason. They've been focusing on harrying us instead of committing to any decisive attacks. They want to keep Orario's forces outside the walls."

According to him, the enemy's real aim was *inside the city*.

No one questioned the wise captain's decision. It was imperative for some of the familias to return to the city in order to avoid playing into the enemy's hand. When the Guild heard Finn's analysis of the situation, they would understand. Surely they would call back some of their forces without delay. *Loki Familia* had their justification for the move.

They had left a decisive-enough impact on the battlefront on the first day, so as long as *Freya Familia* and *Ganesha Familia* stayed, it would be more than enough to handle what was left. It was rather convenient how Loki's plan ended up pushing all the annoying stuff onto Freya, who she was always quarrelling with, as well as her familia.

Loki Familia quickly withdrew from the field, leaving behind their battle standard to convince the enemy they were still there.

Later that evening, they reached Orario.

"We can't prepare for the Evils while fighting a war. If our operations against the Rakian forces drag on much longer, we won't be able to find them."

They passed through the giant city walls at sunset, earning looks of surprise and suspicion from the populace. Finn gathered the familia in the plaza before the city gate to brief them on the plan going forward.

"Riveria and I will take care of handling the spies Rakia has probably snuck into the city. The rest of you should continue the search for information about the key...but also rest up a bit. You've probably strained yourselves a bit participating in the war, since that's not our usual job, and we haven't had a break in half a month. Raul, gather all the requests for time off. I'll take care of scheduling them."

"Got it!"

After that, the various members dispersed to enjoy their brief respite.

Far from the battlefield, and right before they got back to Orario.

Gareth and a handful of people had separated from the main group and started inspecting the area surrounding the city.

"Found it!"

"Th-there really was one..."

They were on a rocky outcropping over four kirlos away from the city.

Stepping into an inconspicuous cave close enough to the coast to see the waves, the adventurers found a man-made passage hewn into the natural rock.

"When I heard they were moving those man-eating flowers into Meren, I thought this might be the case. Small or even middling ones I could see, but getting big ones out via the city gate would be too suspicious. Even with the cooperation of *Ishtar Familia* and other mercantile groups."

Gareth's group had taken a different path after they were released from dealing with Rakia. If they reentered the city, it would be an incredibly tedious process to get back out again, so in order to take care of the familia's current objective of gathering information about Knossos, they intended to look from the outside for any underground passages out of the city.

"They got Knossos's man-eating flowers out from here..." The chienthrope Cruz was dumbfounded.

"They can also bring in food and supplies. Not to mention all the resources to create the labyrinth..."

"Another route in and out that could avoid inspection by the city, you mean?"

"Aye. The Rakian spies Finn was suspicious of might be using it, too."

It was also possible that in the past, the Evils had used it to raise money, charging a high toll to let outlaws into the city.

Raising a magic-stone lantern, the Level-4 Cruz stared down the man-made passage.

"Still, it's amazing we found it…Honestly, when I heard we were going to be searching every nook and cranny around the city, I got dizzy just thinking about it."

"It's not like we're just turning over any old rocks looking for it. Examining the ground's a dwarf's specialty. If nothing else, I've got experience!"

Before he came to Orario, long before he met Loki and Finn and joined the familia, Gareth worked as a miner of coal and ore in his homeland. He had set out for dangerous volcanoes and found countless veins of precious metals. And of course, he had been involved in the construction of countless tunnels. Based on Knossos's estimated scale, the size of Orario, and then the need for discretion, he had zeroed in on this location.

"Let's destroy this. Can any of you lads use explosive magic?"

"Y-yes!"

"Then torch it. This'll cut off their main supply line. Since Knossos is connected to the city and the Dungeon, it's just a minor setback for them, though…After we're done here, we're gonna make sure there aren't any other routes in. North, south, east, and west, we're goin' over all of Orario's surroundings with a fine-tooth comb."

"*Gaaah*…Understood."

While *Loki Familia*'s few male members began to chant, Cruz steeled himself unhappily. The Labyrinth City itself was huge; the area of its surroundings was immeasurable.

Their break would have to wait for now.

"Sorry, Bete Loga, but it isn't here, eitheeer."

"Feh…A big waste of time, huh?"

The curtain of night had fallen on Orario. In the moonlit southeast quarter of the city, people were going about their business in the restored part of the Pleasure Quarter. The night they had returned to the city, Bete and a group from *Loki Familia* were searching for the key. He had dragged Lena, formerly of *Ishtar Familia*, away from the war front to show him where the key was, as she had promised. They were in Belit Babili, Ishtar's home.

"Looks like the Evils got here first...But there's no trail. I can't smell those assholes at all."

"Yeah, there's no signs of a struggle, either. Maybe Ishtar or another familia member who knew about it already took it?"

They were inside a hidden room connected to Ishtar's inner sanctum. There were golden crowns and gorgeous veils glittering with stardust adorning the shelves and wardrobes, but Daedalus's Orb was nowhere to be found. The small box on top of the table that Lena had seen was empty. Aggravated at Lena, Bete tore the room up, looking high and low for it before turning to glare back at her.

"Beeete, I searched that Tammuz guy's room, but I couldn't find it. Sheesh, I want some overtime."

"Overtime, my ass! You probably just did a half-assed check. Stupid Amazon."

"Like I'd do that!"

"Aki and the animal-person kid helped out. We checked everywhere, but there wasn't a hidden room or anything."

Tiona and Tione and the others had met up with them in the goddess's sanctum.

Bete scoffed as their report killed his last hope at a lead.

"Back to the drawing board again. Would have been nice to get the key that Valletta what's-her-face had."

"Bete blew them all away, though."

"...What, is it my fault, huh?"

He hadn't just blown them away; he'd incinerated them. He sullenly avoided eye contact. The reality was that even if they wanted to search for the key belonging to the commander of their newly resurfaced enemy, there were no leads to follow.

They hadn't witnessed it themselves, but knowing how enraged he was at the time, they wouldn't be so insensitive as to blame him for not pressing Valletta Grede for the key's location, but…

"Quit it! Don't blame Bete! It's all my fault!"

For some reason, Lena's cheeks were flushed as she excitedly covered for Bete.

"It's just that when he thought they had killed me, he swore to get revenge for me but…Hee-hee-hee-hee…I guess that's love. Love?! Proof Bete loves me!"

"Shut your damn mouth or I'll shut it for you!"

"What?! My mouth…with Bete Loga's mouth?! Yaaah! So bold! But if you say so, dear. Mmmm~."

Lena closed her eyes and pursed her lips only to be struck in the cheek by Bete's clenched fist.

"*Gyaaaaaaaaaaaaaaaaaaaaaa?!*"

"I'll kill you, you delusional twit."

"Could you quit acting so lovey-dovey? It's an eyesore."

"Why are you getting jealous, Tione?!"

Lena rolled on the ground, holding her cheek, while Bete seemed about ready to burst a vein. Tione seemed even more murderous than the werewolf as she watched her fellow Amazon flirt (that's how it appeared from her perspective), while Tiona desperately pinned her older sister's fists behind her back.

As the room instantly descended into chaos, the catgirl Anakity and the others sighed.

"Lefiya…Was it here?"

"Yes, Miss Aiz…"

The eighteenth floor of the Dungeon. Aiz, Lefiya, Narfi, and a few others were in the area just outside the great forest.

The grove of blue crystals reminiscent of ancient stone circles sparked Lefiya's memory. Around one and a half months ago, she had run into Bell by chance and gotten involved in a fight with a trap monster while chasing some Evils' Remnants. At the time, she wasn't able to catch them in the confusion, so she didn't get any information, but now that they knew of the existence of Knossos, *Loki Familia* came back to reinvestigate.

Standing at the edge of the forest, they saw a giant rock wall towering above them and marking the end of the floor. They began searching the area.

"..."

"Miss Aiz?"

"Here…They tried to cover it, but this patch of ground has been walked on a lot more than everywhere else."

Leaning over with her hand against the wall, the first-tier adventurer dug at the ground a bit and elaborated in her usual few words. As nervous as the rest of the group, Lefiya stepped forward and let loose an Arcs Ray. The rock wall's face broke apart with ease, revealing an inner cavern. Beyond that stood a giant metal gate.

"An orichalcum door!"

"Yeah, we found it…"

The others whispered among themselves as Aiz stared fixedly at it.

They had found the once hypothetical route connecting Knossos and the Dungeon. Suddenly tense, they carefully began examining the cavern and the door blocking the passageway, on guard for a surprise attack from the enemy.

"This is how the Evils' Remnants brought the man-eating flowers aboveground, isn't it…?"

"Maybe? There might be other doors connecting to the Dungeon…"

Aiz reminded Lefiya of the possibility of more routes between the Dungeon and Knossos. However, from this, they could confirm that Knossos at least went as far down as the eighteenth floor, the middle levels. They had confirmed Finn's prediction. Lefiya and the others were once again awed by the ominous man-made labyrinth.

"Miss Aiz, it looks like we won't find the key. What shall we do? Leave a lookout to watch for anyone going in or out?"

"…Mm, we probably shouldn't. Most likely, they already know… that we came here…"

After Narfi finished examining the door and delivered her report, Aiz shook her head.

She looked at the things on either side of the gate: sculptures of devils. Their stone eyes hid a dim blue light. It was probably the same technology as the surveillance "eye" that had been used to operate the door from afar and separate *Loki Familia* when they had wandered into the man-made labyrinth before.

Leaving a lookout here would not help them find anything, and haphazardly splitting their forces would just needlessly increase the risk of being attacked. The others grimaced and backed away from the door, understanding Aiz's implication. The wall was quickly regenerating as they moved, and before long the entrance in the rock face was covered over again.

"We should report this to Finn. But first, look around the area…a little…"

"Yes, we should search to see if there is anything else first."

Despite Aiz's clumsiness with words, which should have been a fatal flaw for one of a familia's commanders, the group split up to carry out her order. The golden-haired, golden-eyed girl furrowed her brow apologetically, blushing a little bit as the others smiled. That was just one side of her they loved.

In any case, they had at least accomplished something. They had not found the key that they needed to take it on, but *Loki Familia* was closing in on Knossos, slowly but surely.

"Lefiya…There was a time…you ran into Bell, right?"

"Y-yes, Miss Aiz. And after that, a masked adventurer saved us…"

"Masked adventurer…"

Searching together with Aiz, Lefiya paused to wipe off some sweat.

They had spread out around the forest and the stone circle under the white crystal light shining down from the ceiling. Squinting slightly in the sunlight filtered through the trees, Lefiya stole a glance at Aiz as she looked around the area.

I heard Lady Riveria's story of Aiz's past, but…Ahhhhh, I still cannot really believe it. A willful, childish Aiz…

Lefiya mulled over the story she'd heard from Riveria that night at the camp.

Mischievous, freer with her emotions than she was now, unreliable… It was an unimaginable story given the beautiful, awe-inspiring swords-woman standing before her now. She could not believe her ears when she heard it.

Ahhh, but I would have liked to see a cute little seven-year-old Miss Aiz with a tooth missing! Oh, if I ask Loki, maybe she'll let me see that baby tooth…Wait, what am I getting excited about?! I'm not some p-p-p-pervert…!

"What is it…Lefiya?"

"Ahhh?!"

Lefiya frantically snapped back to reality when Aiz turned to check on her. She briefly feared that Aiz had figured out the day-dream she was having, and she quickly tried to hide the truth.

"Ah, um, that is…For some reason, Lady Riveria told me that I resembled how you used to be, so I was just looking at you a bit… Ah-ha-ha-ha!"

Eh? Lefiya thought as Aiz stared intently at her.

Holding her gaze, Aiz closed in until they were nearly nose-to-nose.

"U-ummm…"

"…"

She examined the shocked elf's face, then gently grabbed her left hand and examined that too, then caressed her silky golden-yellow hair. Aiz's hand moved down, checking her clothes and staff and all her equipment, before she finally nodded.

"Yeah…it's fine."

"I-it's fine…?"

"You're…taking much better care of yourself than I did."

"Eh?"

"You're nothing like how I was."

With that, Aiz smiled just a little bit.

Lefiya was shocked—she had never seen the younger Aiz's smile, but for some reason, she could imagine it looking like that.

She was at a loss for words.

The smile wasn't particularly self-deprecating, but she felt like Aiz meant exactly what she said. But she could not understand why Aiz mentioned it, and that perplexed her.

In the end, Lefiya couldn't find any words to say before they left the floor along with everyone else.

While her followers were running around, the patron goddess made some moves of her own.

"That dumbass Ares should know how strong we are by now. Just quit it alreadyyy."

Swallowing a yawn, Loki took in the scenery with a bored look.

Placing her arms on the armrest of her seat, the Goddess of Beauty next to her leaned forward slightly.

"So, changin' the topic a bit, Freya."

"Why so serious all of a sudden?"

"...Ya know a child by the name'a Tammuz?"

Wails echoed around the battlefield as Loki confronted Freya with a sharp question.

Facing forward, the silver-haired goddess was silent for a moment before turning her silver eyes to meet Loki's gaze.

"...Did this child do something?"

"Don't dodge the question. Ya know 'im or not?"

"I haven't the slightest clue what you're getting at, Loki. Without understanding your intent, all I can say is I don't know."

The familia members guarding the pair instantly got nervous at the sudden frosty exchange. As both sides watched each other, on guard for attempts to harm their familia's patron goddess, Loki responded as if she had expected Freya's answer all along.

"Because of that pain-in-the-ass fight you had with Ishtar, her vice captain went missing. I wanna know where he went."

"Why are you asking me?"

"The day he disappeared, the ones tearin' up the Pleasure District were your children. It's normal to check if you had seen him, or had seen him get killed, or if you're *hiding* him."

"Why are you after that child?"

"I'm lookin' for somethin', ya see. A kinda creepy magic item, got weird symbols inscribed in it."

"…"

"Ishtar had it, but now that she's back in Heaven, I was wondering if her second-in-command might've taken it…Just covering my bases."

The location of *Ishtar Familia*'s vice captain, Tammuz Berrilli, and the whereabouts of the key to Knossos.

Loki was using the impending war with Rakia to visit, intent on pinning those pieces of information down. It was all in order to corner the capricious Goddess of Beauty who always seemed to elude contact.

Freya recognized that discussing the conflict with Rakia was not really the point, and that Loki had come here specifically for a chance to meet her in person.

"Hypothetically, Loki…" She started speaking, maintaining her calm, composed demeanor. "Hypothetically, if that child you were talking about *happened to suit my tastes*…and I can't imagine why, but if *someone happened to be coming after him…*"

"…"

"Do you think that I would carelessly reveal that child's location?"

Freya ruled over beauty and love. She would protect the children she favored no matter what, and regardless of the consequences, she wouldn't allow anyone to take them away from her.

That was the message hidden behind Freya's smile.

So that's how it was.

"But yes. If I find anything out, I'll let you know…probably."

However, she could not flat-out reject Loki. As if announcing the end of the conversation, she turned away from the goddess who wielded the same status and military strength as she did.

In response, Loki swung her legs up and rose to her feet.

"Welp, guess that's how it goes. Finding out he's being shielded by the most annoying woman possible's still something, at least."

"Oh-ho, what on Earth could you be referring to?"

"But I should tell you, if you pull your usual queenly act, there won't be any taking it back."

"Oh my. Is that a threat?"

"Just the truth. Before you know it, your castle might get *blown away*…And if it does, I'll be the one pointin' and laughin'."

Loki snorted disgustedly before leaving with her guard. The trickster goddess departed quickly as Freya silently stared at her.

That conversation had taken place on the first day of the war.

"Loki is looking for Tammuz…"

They were now in *Freya Familia*'s camp in the fields outside the city. Freya was inside her giant tent, reflecting on the events from a few days before. Sitting on her seat, she asked the person before her:

"*Tammuz*, tell me again. What was Ishtar planning?"

"Y-yes, my lady. Ishtar had reached out to *Kali Familia* and even the Evils' Remnants in order to defeat you. She wanted to lure Warlord and the rest into Knossos to strike them down with the demi-spirits…"

The kneeling dark-skinned, black-haired man answered the beautiful goddess as his cheeks flushed.

As Freya listened to him, she fiddled with the metal orb inscribed with the symbol *D* in her right hand—Daedalus's Orb.

The day that her familia destroyed the Pleasure Quarter, she had charmed the defeated goddess's favored child. She stole him away while Ishtar herself watched. Just as Loki suspected, *Freya Familia* was hiding him.

At first it had been merely curiosity. She had brought him back to their home in order to find out why Ishtar was willing to use any method possible to take her down. But after a few days, *someone had tried to kill him*. A mysterious guest had invaded her castle in an assassination attempt.

Strong, beautiful, and loyal, Tammuz had already piqued Freya's interest and received her favor. There was no way the Goddess of Beauty would willingly hand over one of her children. To protect him, she had Ottar and a couple of others dispose of the assassins. Thoroughly, in order to prevent any more information leaking out.

Freya had not revealed anything to Loki in order to protect her follower, but at the same time...she clearly understood why he was being targeted.

It was because of the key he had taken with him when *Ishtar Familia* had been destroyed.

"The Evils' Remnants, Knossos, demi-spirits..."

She examined the key glinting in the light of the magic-stone lamps, her full lips repeating the information Tammuz had given her.

"It seems things have gotten interesting while I wasn't paying attention."

"What shall we do, Freya?"

Stationed beside her throne, the boaz warrior Ottar solemnly awaited his mistress's commands.

Despite receiving the keyword, she could not connect everything with only Tammuz's information. She was silent for a moment before responding.

"I would like to determine whether something is happening in Orario at the moment."

"Should I contact *Loki Familia*?"

"No. If we exchange information with Loki, she will no doubt demand this key."

She smiled bewitchingly as Ottar looked up at her.

"I suspect holding on to this for the moment will be better...That's merely what my intuition is telling me, though."

Of course, the intuition she mentioned was the intuition of a divine being. She rose from her throne.

"Call Allen for me. I'll have him go back to the city."

"I've got a reward lined up, so find me that magic item."

The first words out of Loki's mouth upon entering a certain familia's home were directed at the god before her eyes.

"That's rather abrupt. We've formed an alliance, haven't we? Could you tell me what it is?"

Hermes grinned as he held up Finn's sketch of Daedalus's Orb. It fluttered in the air as he shook his hand questioningly.

They were meeting in *Hermes Familia*'s home, the Traveler's Lodge. The war was still raging outside the city, but Loki had returned to Orario and marched into Hermes's base without even a bodyguard, causing a stir among Asfi, Lulune, and his other followers.

"And this after you didn't tell me about Daedalus Street. You investigated it like we discussed, right? When I asked Dionysus about it, he wouldn't tell me anything."

"You were the one Dionysus said to watch out for, after all."

"Come on now. I'm Hermes! I've got nothing to hide."

"You were the reason Freya wrecked Ishtar's place, weren't ya?"

"…"

Ignoring his jokes, Loki pressed harder. Hermes smiled, raising his hands as if surrendering, but he neither confirmed nor denied her accusation.

"It's a bit late for me to be gettin' suspicious, but Dionysus ain't the only one with doubts about you. What is Uranus hidin'? What's he plannin'?"

"Who knows? We get a lot of contracts from the Guild, but… it's not like they totally trust us, either. Ouranos doesn't tell me everything."

Not *everything*.

Loki really wanted to smash her fist into the jaw of the god sitting across the desk from her.

—*Sheesh, they're all damn foxes who won't show their hands.*

"If you're gonna play dumb, then we'll keep quiet about what we've found as well."

"Well, that's a problem, since I really don't know anything."

"Yeah, yeah. But—if you happen to find this magic item, bring it to me, and I'll share what I know."

Them's the terms.

Hermes Familia was a Dungeon-crawling familia, but they also made a living by working in several other industries like negotiations and information brokering. They were good at what they did and maintained their neutrality. If something needed to be found, there was no place better to send the job.

Ouranos's ulterior motives or the key's whereabouts. One or the other. That was what Loki was demanding.

Hermes looked down at the parchment sketch again.

"If you're calling it a commission, then we'll take it, but…Got any leads to start with?"

"Nope. It's somewhere in the city."

"Come on now. That's a bit much, don't you think?"

"Oh yeah. There might be a lead at Freya's place. There ya go—somewhere to start. Deal with it."

"H-hey now. You sound like you're just telling me to go die in a fire."

Hermes's face actually twitched at that last comment. Loki stuck out her tongue as Hermes started to break into a sweat.

"If ya want my trust, then ya gotta do that much, at least. Oh yeah, I forgot to mention, but there's more than one of those magic items. Anyway, I'm countin' on you."

Finishing everything she had come to say, Loki quickly took her leave.

The war tiger and the prum girl glanced around in confusion as she left their home.

After Loki was gone, Hermes sighed slightly and turned to his followers standing behind him.

"Oh boy…It's rough being stuck between a rock and a hard place."

Now you say that?

Asfi and Lulune merely snorted at the dandy god.

Days passed.

As the encirclement of Knossos steadily progressed, *Loki Familia* had a real sense that they were closing in on the creatures and remnants of the Evils holed up there. However, time mercilessly flowed on while they remained unable to open the way in. The passage of time was not merely beneficial to the enemy. If this went on too long, it would bring about the collapse of Orario itself. Lefiya and the others were getting impatient. They were one move away. If only they could just get one step further on this front. That was the kind of atmosphere that hung thick around *Loki Familia*.

On the other hand, things with Rakia were rapidly headed for a conclusion. Thanks to Finn's arrangements, they had received word that *Ares Familia*'s spies had been captured. He had shared the information with *Hephaistos Familia* and asked for assistance, so they ended up with the glory, but in *Loki Familia*, he was greeted by cheers of "That's our captain!" with Tione leading the call.

"But the people of the city have no clue about that."

Lefiya murmured to herself as she walked through the streets. It was late morning, and the sky was clear and blue.

Because the Guild loathed unnecessary confusion, the existence of the spies was not made public. Apparently, there had been quite a few of them, and they had even brought in a certain legendary magic item—one of Crozzo's Magic Swords. If there had been any mistake, an entire block might have gone up in flames, but there was no telling that from the peaceful hustle and bustle of the city.

Rakia did not have any other cards left to play, so the war outside the city would be cleared up soon. That was what they believed, and then they would finally be able to seriously start dealing with the Evils.

Currently she was out gathering information during her shopping trip for the familia.

"Hey, did you hear? The Little Rookie beat a floor boss. Or at least I heard it was some kind of insane beast!"

"I guess his victory in the War Game wasn't a fluke."

"Yeah, we might be seeing the birth of another amazing adventurer."

"G-grrr..."

Lefiya groaned a bit. Instead of the news about Rakian spies getting rounded up, the Little Rookie was the talk of the town. In the shops, in the markets, among passersby, all she heard was chatter about his feats.

It had not even been a month since the War Game, and the

excitement had not passed yet. Everyone was talking about the instantly famous super rookie and how they had high expectations for him.

I'm here doing all I can, and he is just hopping around for attention…!

For Lefiya, who was going through a lot of trial and error in her quest to become strong, his fame was practically taunting her. It wasn't as though he had any bad intentions, but to her, it felt like while she was struggling up the slope, the person next to her was easily springing up by leaps and bounds like a rabbit.

Lefiya felt her insides churning from a combination of regret and jealousy.

…But I think I get it.

Suddenly, a tinge of understanding appeared on her face. She knew why Aiz had started training him. She had wanted to understand the secret to his crazy rate of growth.

The kind and serious girl instinctively thought that compensation for the training would be selfish and had sincerely answered the boy's request for mentorship.

Lefiya, after hearing she resembled how Aiz used to be, had a hunch that she might understand what Aiz had felt at the time.

"It's aggravating…really, really aggravating, but…I should try asking, too."

Right as she was saying that to herself—

"Ah."

"Ah."

Turning the corner, she unexpectedly bumped into the boy himself. The white-haired, red-eyed boy, Bell Cranell.

"Lefiya?"

"Wh-wh-wh-why are you here?!"

"Um, I just happened to be walking past, is all…"

She was shaken by the sudden encounter, but when they were both in the same neighborhood, encountering each other in the street wasn't that strange.

Lefiya was at a loss for words, but Bell did not seem to mind as he soon asked a question.

"Um, you wouldn't happen to have seen the goddess—Hestia, would you?"

"Hestia…you mean your patron deity?"

"Yes, she left our home, so I was looking for her."

If he was asking someone who viewed him as a rival, then something must have happened. It was easy enough to guess from the light sweat on his face that he had been searching all over town.

The goddess Hestia. Lefiya had not had any direct interactions with her, but Lefiya knew of her. Her patron goddess, Loki, was often bad-mouthing her. And Lefiya had also caught glimpses of her working at the Jyaga Maru Kun shop.

"I haven't seen her…Did something happen?"

"Ah, no. That is…We just had a little fight, kind of."

Lefiya's voice finally came back. Her curiosity was piqued as Bell's gaze darted around in embarrassment. Lefiya blinked.

"That's unexpected…I thought you were bad with women. The sort of person who gets lovestruck and can't stand his ground."

"Gah?!"

He was almost pathetically taken aback, indicating her words had struck home.

She remembered when they first met. When they bumped into each other then, as soon as he found out she was an elf, he turned to mush, unable to calm down as he flushed red.

Now she held a grudge against him for various crimes related to Aiz, but at the time, she had thought he was modest and unsophisticated. A fight between him and a beautiful goddess was entirely unexpected.

His rubellite eyes looked clouded over, as if with unspoken emotions, and his expression was dark.

"…Was it really just a fight?"

"H-how did you know?"

What do you mean, how…?

Lefiya dubiously raised an eyebrow as he struggled to find the words. Looking at him now, anyone could tell he was worried about something. That was how easy he was to read.

Sighing slightly, Lefiya responded.

"If I see Hestia, I'll let you know."

"Eh?"

"You are worried, right? I'm saying I will help you."

"Th-that's...I couldn't bother you. And besides, you...um, don't really..."

"I'm not sure what you think I am. While it is true that I dislike you, I have enough of a heart to help people who are in trouble! And you can be sure I'll get my compensation from you later."

Yes, just like Aiz.

She was not a saint. If she managed to help him find Hestia, then she could ask him for the secret to his growth. Lefiya would simply be helping Bell in order to create an excuse to learn that.

"Th-thank you very much!"

"...It's not that big a deal."

Turning away from Bell as he thanked her, she felt a flush of heat rise in her cheeks from his straightforwardness.

After he had bowed more times than she could count, Lefiya headed for the city's western quarter to look for information about the key and maybe track down the goddess's whereabouts.

Searching for a magic item in the giant Labyrinth City and finding a single goddess were both difficult propositions. But for the latter, there was at least a chance someone might have seen her. Lefiya traveled along the high-traffic Main Street and asked around.

Dark clouds...And it was clear before. It might rain.

Inside the tall city walls, she could see a mass of gray clouds to the north. With the darkening sky urging her onward, she naturally sped up.

A little while after she ran into the boy, she found out that the childish goddess had wandered to the north of the city. At that moment, Orario's usual liveliness suddenly changed.

"...? The city feels more panicked...?"

Her elf ears reacted. There was something out of place among the sounds of the city's usual bustling noise. An animal person ran through the market looking pale, grabbing people all the while to spread some piece of news. Human shopkeepers were huddled together, whispering and pointing in the same direction. Adventurers and Guild employees ran past without a sidelong glance.

Lefiya looked where they were heading—to the north.

"Did something…happen?"

Feeling the city's growing restlessness, Lefiya was about to head north herself when—

"Lefiya!"

"Miss Tione, Miss Tiona?!"

"Lefiya, it's big trouble!"

She ran into the Amazons dashing from the side street.

They had Urga and Zolas equipped. Lefiya finally realized that something really big was going on.

"Did something happen?!"

"Rakia's last-ditch attack!"

"For some reason, they appeared at the city's north gate, and rumor has it they managed to kidnap a goddess."

Lefiya was horrified.

The situation wasn't exactly clear, either, because they had only just learned of the events themselves, but apparently all available Guild members and adventurers were assembling at the north gate.

"Wh-which goddess was kidnapped?!"

"It was little Argonaut's goddess, they said…"

"Wh…? Hestia?!"

"Yes. And they've already dispatched an emergency rescue squad with—"

Lefiya was dumbstruck by what was unfolding around her, but Tione continued without letting her get a word in edgewise.

"*E-EHHHHHHHHHHHHHHHHHHHHHHHHHHHHHHHHHHH?!*"

And when she heard the last bit of news, she screamed.

"…"

Riveria's gaze dropped to the book open before her.

She was in Twilight Manor's office. The members were in the middle of getting ready to leave, while she found herself looking over *Loki Familia*'s records that Finn maintained with great care.

Ever since they had established themselves in Orario, he had kept track of the familia's history, recording the people in their rosters and the depth they reached in the Dungeon, as well as details like their levels. Of course, secret things like magic and skills and the like were not recorded, but the growth and efforts of their comrades were described there. It was a vivid testament to Finn's dedication to running the faction effectively.

Among the many records, Riveria eventually reached one girl's past.

"Danger lurking." "Needs company to enter the Dungeon." "Something shines in her swordsmanship." "Gareth and I may have trained her too well." "Even if she had an escort, getting to floor 10 solo in half a year is amazing." And on and on...She laughed slightly at the journal-like notes Finn had left in the margins of the records.

It was not the first time she had taken several of the thick record books off the shelf and opened them on the desk.

Abruptly, she took off the hair band pulling her hair back.

She peered at the golden hair band in her hands as her long, pale jade hair flowed like a clear forest stream down her back.

"Oh, Riveria. Ye were in here?"

Gareth had been passing by the open door when he saw her and entered.

"Gareth, you're back? What is it?"

"Do you have any Alb's Pure Water? This stain's stubborn. I've a feeling I won't be able to get it out without it."

Gareth held a sheathed shortsword in his hand. Pulling it out revealed a nicked and battered blade. It was a rare piece with a visible wave running the length of the blade. It was noticeably dirty, giving it a sense of age, but it was clear from the luster that the blade's edge had not dulled yet.

"That sword...You were holding on to it, Gareth?"

"I suppose. It was a special occasion, so I decided to take it. Finn said to take a break, but I've got nothing I want to do, and it was starting to get dark…Then all of a sudden, I remembered this."

Having just returned to Orario after going around destroying the entrances to Knossos outside the city, the dwarf lifted up the short-sword he had brought from his room.

"For some reason, I got the urge to give it a good polish."

Gareth's eyes turned warm as if he was remembering something as he examined the damaged sword.

"What about you? You're letting your hair down when you're not going to bed. It's been a while since I've seen you do that."

Gareth glanced up at her. Riveria was silent for a moment, staring at the hair band in her hand.

"The other day…I told Lefiya a story from Aiz's past."

"Oh?"

"It's not just that, though…I've found myself reflecting on what happened back then. It's rather unlike me, but I've been feeling sentimental lately."

Hearing that much, Gareth stroked his beard, as if agreeing with her.

"Ga-ha-ha! That's just how it goes. I'm the same, after all. We probably think back on the past because the fighting is so intense now. If we die, we won't be able to do that, either."

"Don't say something so ominous, Gareth."

Riveria glanced down at him, but he just smiled back at her warning.

"Perhaps we're the ones who can't let go of her."

"…"

"Well, Aiz's become a perfectly competent adventurer. She's gradually stopped being such a handful for us—"

Just as he said that, the sound of hurried footsteps echoed from the hallway, and someone rushed into the office.

"Riveria! Gareth!"

"Alicia? What is it?"

They both turned to the ashen elf who had rushed into the room.

The second-tier adventurer breathlessly delivered her report.

"Aiz has left the city in order to track Rakia's detached forces! It seems she's headed toward the Beor Mountain Range with Little Rookie!"

Their eyes filled with shock, and they both whirled around to look out the office's window. The sky to the north was filled with dark clouds extending out to the mountain range—lightning struck in the distance, and the thunderclap rolled over Orario.

"…The Beor Mountain Range…in poor weather…I've a bad feeling about this."

"Yes…At the very least, we can't afford to make any assumptions about the situation…What a mess."

Riveria responded to the dwarf as they both furrowed their brows.

They quickly set off. Bringing Alicia with them, they left the office.

The two moved through the hall quickly in order to meet up with Finn, who had taken command of the operation. Riveria sighed slightly.

"She's still quite the handful."

RECOLLECTIONS
CHAPTER
2

ARE YOU A
SWORD
?

Гэта казка іншага сям

Ты Нары Уа меч

Aiz Wallenstein

LEVEL 1

Strength: E489 -> D502 Endurance: E434 -> 438
Dexterity: D597 -> C605 Agility: C606 -> 615 Magic: I0

Riveria looked at the girl's updated Status's numbers and sighed.

"Half a year since becoming an adventurer…That's an impressive rate of growth."

"I knew she had potential, but to come this far…"

Finn smiled wryly after she handed him the sheet that had been translated into Koine.

Loki had updated Aiz's Status first thing that morning, and she had informed Finn and Riveria once they returned to the manor after finishing a mission for the Guild.

"At this rate, she's headed for a pretty crazy level-up. Far as the familia's concerned, it's all sunshine and rainbows…But as for Aiz herself, I'm not too happy about this."

The familia's patron goddess sat cross-legged on top of the office's desk.

"Yes…With how she's been wearing herself down, that's to be expected."

"She's constantly asking for more training with Finn and Gareth, and she's been serious about her studies. She has largely learned to control her emotions, but…that girl still does not take care of herself. Training, training, training. Always training."

"She's only learned some of how to handle herself in a fight, but it was enough to let her brute-force her way a little. I might have been a bit premature giving her permission to go into the Dungeon."

"That said, with the Evils runnin' rampant in the city nowadays, it'd be a problem if Aizuu didn't keep gettin' stronger, either. It's not like y'all will always be around to protect her."

The fact that Aiz did not pay any heed to the toll on her body was bothering them. The first-tier adventurers had no complaints about her desire to learn more and more from them, but she was too impatient. To put it bluntly, she refused to pay attention to anything other than becoming stronger.

There was plenty of blame to go around, though. Finn and Gareth had seen a spark of something in her techniques and then witnessed her joy at receiving instruction, which eventually led them to unwittingly teach her too much.

"Do you know what the lower-class adventurers call Aiz now?"

"What?"

"It's a riot. She's the Doll Princess."

"I'm not laughing."

"Seriously. Our Aizuu is waaay cuter and more huggable than any doll!"

"That's not what they mean."

Riveria felt her frustration rise a notch and stared at the ceiling after Loki's joke.

"Anyone who keeps plungin' ahead without rest eventually falls on their face…Not that we can get that through to her, though…"

Her quiet confession resonated in the office as Finn and Riveria nodded in silent agreement.

The second hand on the big grandfather clock that Loki had bought on a whim ticked audibly. Finally, Riveria spoke up.

"What is Aiz doing?"

Loki just shrugged and smiled wryly.

"Dungeon, what else? Gareth's taking care of her."

"Gishaaaaaaaaa?!"

A monster howled its dying cry as a single slash of a sword sliced into it.

Without waiting for the purple moth's severed body and wings to hit the floor, Aiz landed and charged on to the next prey.

"—!"

"Gegaaah?!"

The sword's edge neatly ran through the gap in the killer ant's exoskeleton. She struck it at one of the few joints in its carapace. A spray of blood gushed from the giant ant monster's soft interior. As it faltered, she landed a second strike, effortlessly slaying it.

"Aiz, don't be so reckless! Come back for a moment!"

"I can keep going!"

Ignoring Gareth as he defeated a monster to the side, Aiz advanced, her long golden hair fluttering in the air.

The armor she had equipped was a prum armor dress, a grade above the Guild-provided gear she used to wear. The sword she held was a steel shortsword purchased from a weapons store. The former had been modified to match Loki's tastes; the latter Gareth had given to her after using his judgment to pick it out. Armed with those two items, Aiz dove straight into the swarm of monsters. The way she used her small body to close the distance and gain the upper hand against them was reminiscent of a quadruped on the prowl.

Her movements had become unimaginably polished in half a year. It was almost unrecognizable compared to when she used to rely on only brute force and overkilling things left and right. She cut down on the unnecessary movements and power, using her speed and precision to take out the monsters. Using the information she had learned about her enemies, she hit their weak point with greater precision than ever: Since her current targets didn't have a proper head, she simply sliced into the magic stone in their chests.

It was all the product of their lessons. Aiz was gradually developing her own fighting style: a preemptive frontal charge coupled with speedy slashes. However, that gave them one more thing to worry about.

"Her defense is all over the place…Sheesh, she's really only thinkin' about defeating them."

A killer ant's counterattack cut her cheek, but Aiz paid it no heed as she thrust her sword in retaliation. The leather and white metal plates of her armor dress bore countless nicks and scratches from monster claws and teeth. By accepting that damage, though, Aiz was able to unleash twice as many attacks of her own.

She despised defense and disregarded it because she considered it inefficient. Gareth was left troubled as he watched her fight unfold.

Coincidentally, at the same time as Riveria and the others were worrying about her, the girl was ignoring the pain and simply continuing to swing her sword.

"Ngh…!"

"Good grief, you've destroyed another weapon."

Right as the last monster hit the ground, her steel sword cracked before shattering into pieces. Aiz's muted expression shifted, her eyebrows scrunching a bit. Gareth groaned.

"Aiz, you need to account for your own body and take better care of it. Eventually, the bill comes due."

"…I can win against the monsters. It's fine."

"I'm not talkin' about winnin' and losin' here…"

Aiz turned away, wiping the blood dripping down her cheek. Gareth could only sigh. But he declined to push any further as he collected the magic stones and drop items.

Among the three of them, Aiz preferred Gareth's company to the rest.

They hadn't yet known each other half a year, but the things he taught her were more exciting than the subjects of Finn's lessons and simpler than Riveria's. But more than anything, he did not talk much. She had made becoming strong her ultimate goal, after all, so she was grateful for that.

The dwarf warrior's line of thought appeared to be that pain was just another experience Aiz could benefit from, so he wasn't as fussy as Riveria. And it was so much less stressful for her because of that. Riveria had been scolding her more often lately—and Aiz was rebelling against it—so this was a way for her to maintain her emotional equilibrium.

"Let youngsters make mistakes. And then have them learn from them."

Aiz did not grasp the true meaning behind Gareth's words, but she interpreted it conveniently for herself.

"Gareth, just a little more…"

"No can do; we're headin' back."

He was not going to let her force the matter further.

Cut off before she could even finish, she gave a look of dissatisfaction that only the four of them had seen.

"Unbelievable, breaking swords after only a couple of swings… Look, this is the last one I've got."

Pulling double duty as a supporter, Gareth handed her a spare sword. It was her third one on this trip alone. He grumbled about getting too much practice finding cheap weapons from no-name weapons shops as he handed her a potion, too.

They were on the seventh floor.

Currently, they were holed up in a room that dead-ended off the main route.

Under Gareth's instructions, Aiz had stopped actively hunting monsters and was in the process of reluctantly heading back when she suddenly changed her mind and her expression along with it. The stench of monsters pervaded the passage, which stirred up her desire to battle and to kill.

Aiz was already rather muted, but when she was in the Dungeon, she seemed entirely emotionless. She just kept slaughtering monsters with a frozen expression.

The Doll Princess.

Even when a monster's blood splashed across her face, her expression did not change in the slightest. The other adventurers had given her the nickname half in fear, half in scorn as she continued to do nothing but hunt monsters. In this half a year, the newest member of *Loki Familia* had shaved away at her emotions until there was nothing left in her quest to wipe out all the monsters. She had become something of a legend around the Guild and among the lower-class adventurers. At the same time, though, she was the obvious candidate for super rookie of the year.

"Gareth."

"What?"

"The armor…is getting…tight…"

"Huh, already? No, I suppose around your age is when humans start to mature. We just got it fitted, though. Hmm, I guess we should get it changed."

"I want a custom…weapon, too. One that won't break."

"The little newbie's tryin' to make a joke. Learn how to not break your weapons first."

"…Then let me go to the tenth floor next time."

"That's not happening."

"…Why? I already went there twice before…"

"I heard you got full of yourself and nearly let an orc murder you. You've gotta get permission from Riveria and Finn first."

"…"

On the way back, she verbally sparred with Gareth. He would not go along with what she really wanted, though, and her frustrations showed even more clearly on her face.

Feeling more and more constricted by the limitations placed on her lately, Aiz was turning into a big ball of rebelliousness. It wasn't quite bad enough to call a temper tantrum, but she was visibly sullen and unhappy.

*She seems to act like the young girl she is around the four of us, though…*Gareth observed. *That Doll Princess nickname aside, her rebelliousness ain't much different from when we first met her… Though lately she's been looking especially haggard…*

Watching her from a step back, he felt that despite the muscles she had developed, her arms and legs were scrawny.

"Uwaaaaaaaaaa!"

All of a sudden, several screams erupted from somewhere up ahead.

Aiz sprang into action fast enough to give anyone watching

whiplash as she rushed toward the source of the screams. She arrived at the path that connected to the sixth floor above.

"Gaaah?! Damn it! Don't screw with me!"

"There's too many of them!"

"Someone heeelp!"

A swarm of killer ants was gathering around a handful of parties with different emblems. The lower-class adventurers were having a rough time, since a swarm that size was rarely encountered on the upper levels.

"A swarm of killer ants! Some adventurer messed up and pulled a pass parade?!"

A first-tier adventurer, Gareth could immediately tell what had happened. A killer ant had gotten wounded, panicked, and released pheromones to call for reinforcements. An adventurer's failure to finish the job had escalated into the situation before them.

The pass parade had occurred on the main path and managed to block off the connecting path, leaving them no way to escape. Seeing the agitated monsters, Gareth nearly joined the fray, but then—

"———!"

Aiz dove in headlong without analyzing the situation at all.

"Wait! Aiz!"

Gareth's attempt to stop her fell on deaf ears, drowned out by the cries of the killer ants.

With the adventurers' plight as an excuse, she broke past the limits that Riveria and the others had told her to maintain. Unleashing the full force of her Status, the girl transformed into an angel of destruction. Her face emotionless, her golden eyes filled with an overwhelming desire to kill, she swung her sword like the God of Death's scythe.

"Th-that's *Loki Familia*'s…"

"Golden hair, golden eyes…No mistaking it…"

"Uwah…"

Even as their claws lashed at her, wounded her, drew blood, she slaughtered monster after monster. The adventurers who had asked for help paled, speechless as they watched her fight.

The monsters screeched as shattered exoskeletons burst in the air and severed limbs and heads soared across the passage.

In the midst of the feral attacks, her fierce sword techniques exterminated the swarm of killer ants one by one.

"…A killing doll."

"Doll Princess…No, War Princess."

Someone mumbled as the monsters' blood and lamentations alike disappeared into the battlefield.

Gareth stood by himself, silent, watching the murderous scene that left no room for him to intervene.

"…Done."

Finally, the mountain of corpses was complete.

Standing in the center of the beasts' grave was a bloodstained golden-haired, golden-eyed girl.

The silent corner of the Dungeon was painted red. Since it was along the main route, a great many people witnessed it.

The adventurers were frozen in place, having caught a glimpse and sensed a portion of the girl's madness.

Before their eyes, the girl, covered in wounds, looked up at the ceiling in the labyrinth with no sky.

Finally, cracks ran along her sword, and it shattered into shards like silver raindrops.

"I want a sturdier sword."

Expressionless, Aiz made her demand in a sharp voice.

"Those are the first words out of your mouth right after you come back?"

Riveria massaged her brow, as if trying to soothe a headache.

The office had become a lecture hall. After returning from the Dungeon, Aiz was immediately called in. Even if she hid the wounds using a potion, the stains from all the blood splattered across her armor couldn't be scrubbed away. The elf was furious after hearing the gist of things from Gareth.

That said, Gareth himself seemed unconcerned.

"Aiz, that's enough! Your behavior has been intolerable lately!"

"No...it isn't. I do my studies. I listen to what Gareth and Finn say, too."

"That's not what I'm talking about! You need to take better care of yourself!"

"More importantly, my sword—"

"What do you mean, 'more importantly'?! You think I'll let that slide? Fool!"

It's started again. Gareth looked worn out. Reaching a stopping point in his paperwork, Finn looked on with his now well-practiced wry smile. Loki was away dealing with another issue as Riveria's scolding heated up.

"Don't think it's fine just because you're improving! This is exactly how adventurers who haven't properly developed their abilities get themselves killed! And you went and used your Skill despite what we said! Even after we told you so often not to rely on it and use your normal Status to fight!"

"...Stupid elf."

"What?!"

"Calm down, Riveria."

Gareth tried to soothe Riveria after Aiz's absentmindedly whispered response. The high elf winced as she closed her eyes and took a deep breath. When she opened them again, they were full of hurt.

"...And you've been so focused on training that you haven't been eating properly."

Riveria took Aiz's right arm.

Even taking into account her young age, it was far too scrawny. There was no extraneous flesh at all. Only refined muscle, skin, and bones. Almost swordlike in the way it had been honed for a single goal. Her once beautiful golden hair was in similarly terrible shape.

Aiz was spending literally all her time training. She ate the minimal amount of food required to sustain herself, angled for any chance to steal a moment with Finn or Gareth for a mock battle, and spent all her free time practicing sword swings. Given how early she got up, she was probably losing sleep. She had probably accumulated a tremendous deal of fatigue.

Aiz pulled her arm away from Riveria, an awkward look on her face.

That face had become hollow as well.

Or rather—it had been sharpened.

To a dangerous extent.

Her battered body had definitely gotten stronger, increasing the power she could call upon.

But at this rate, it was almost as if—

"I can fight. So it's okay. More importantly…"

More importantly.

Aiz didn't notice that the moment she said it, Riveria's face contorted in anguish. Her eyes filled with sadness.

Only Finn and Gareth noticed their friend's response.

"I want a weapon that won't break. A weapon that can fight more."

Stepping away from Riveria, Aiz settled her gaze onto Finn, the captain.

He glanced over at Gareth, standing behind the girl. The dwarf was holding the shortsword that had broken in the last fight.

"If money is the problem…I have enough, right? Use all of it…if you need to."

All the things she had gotten from the monsters she defeated were exchanged for money, which was deposited in her savings. Riveria was managing it, though the payments for her items and weapons were deducted accordingly. Even accounting for the necessary costs, Aiz had managed to kill over three thousand in the past six months, so if she used all her savings, it was more than likely she'd get a fairly good weapon. She was sure of that.

However.

"Aiz…I'm in agreement with Riveria. We can't give you a strong weapon when you're in this state."

Finn flatly rejected her request. Glancing back to Aiz, he continued.

"Even if we ignore your current condition, you've gotten so focused on your goal that you can't even notice when the people right in front of you are worried."

Riveria quickly looked away from Aiz.

Aiz did not understand what it meant, but she was also too worked up to think it over.

Why don't they get it? They know how hard I'm working to fulfill my wish. Those were the sorts of thoughts swirling in her heart.

Aiz gritted her teeth, her shoulders quivering, before finally dashing out of the office.

"Oi, Aiz!…Haaah, good grief."

Gareth stroked his beard as she disappeared down the hall.

Back in the office, Riveria bent over, looking down helplessly to avoid meeting Finn's eyes.

"…What was it they said in the Far East at times like this?"

"Ah, I remember that."

Finn's and Gareth's voices hung in the silent room, exchanging glances as they held back a sigh.

"No child knows how dear she is to her parents."

Aiz ran away from the manor via a back door.

A swirl of wildly different emotions crossed her doll-like face as she pumped her arms, trying to escape. She was not just running away, though. She had a goal in mind.

She was headed for Northwest Main Street, also known as Adventurers Way.

I'll find one myself!

An angry glare rising on her face, she let out the full torrent of discontent she had built up at their stubbornness.

Since it had come to this, she decided to find a sword that met her standards on her own.

At this point in time, Aiz was famous, often called the Doll, but she also had some simplistic views and a naughty streak that befit her age. It was particularly striking when she was dealing with Riveria and the others, and how much she despaired when she felt they had abandoned her. It could even be called sulking. The truth was that she had already run away from home like this several times before.

And as per usual, Aiz had set off based purely on emotion.

Requesting a made-to-order weapon from a smithing familia would be best, but...

Perhaps because of her childish nature, Aiz had pressed her face to a certain weapons shop's show window on more than one occasion, staring at the wares on display. But she had also been stunned at the sight of more than seven zeros lined up on the price tags before.

More than anything, though, she did not have any connections with a smithing familia. It was entirely unrealistic.

I guess I have to look for a weapons shop...

The next best alternative was searching for a hidden gem.

Aiz was not a connoisseur, but in the past half a year, she had at least learned which weapons cut well and had good durability. Being able to find a weapon that suited its owner was a crucial skill for adventurers.

Northwest Main Street was a major spot for businesses catering to adventurers. As would be expected of a place called "Adventurers Way," there were countless different specialty shops marketed toward adventurers lining the street. And of course, that included weapons shops.

As for payment, the adventurers' shops would generally be willing to accept a commission if someone showed a familia emblem. Doubly so in her case, since she had the *Loki Familia* emblem. She could arrange the payment from her savings once she had her hands on a sword.

—Think about it later. At that point, Aiz seemed to realize she was no different from a child who insisted on having a certain toy. Bending her values to suit her goal, the seven-year-old girl wanted something special for herself, even if her time as an adventurer influenced what that something would be.

Irritated with the adults who would not let her have her way, she kept rushing ahead without thought.

"...Rain?"

The drops began falling at the worst possible time.

The gray clouds filling the sky had brought a heavy downpour to the city. Normally, Aiz was indifferent to getting drenched, but when the rain started to blow horizontally, even she faltered.

Bedraggled and weather-beaten, she paused her search and fled into the nearest building.

She glared up at the sky, water dripping from her hair, clearly uncomfortable in her soaked clothes.

"—*Waaah.* Man, I'm beat! I could see it was gonna rain, but who knew it'd be this bad?!"

A woman entered the building that Aiz had taken shelter in.

She had a dark complexion and short black hair. Her body was curvaceous in a way that a childlike Aiz could not begin to match, and her voluptuous breasts were just peeking out from her top as she started to undress.

"I have to meet up with the goddess, too…What a disaster."

But most distinctive of all was the jet-black eye patch over her left eye. *Human…No, a half?*

As Aiz focused on her, struggling to determine her race from those characteristics and the general mood about her, the woman wringing out her top finally noticed the girl.

"Oops, someone was already here, huh? And such a cute little girl to boot. Sorry you have to see me like this. You were so small, I didn't notice you!"

"…I'm not small."

The woman was stripping down to just her bra without shame and laughing teasingly. Aiz unconsciously reacted to her bluntness and objected despite only just meeting her.

"I'm sorry; I'm sorry!" The woman laughed before squinting her right eye, examining the girl. Aiz was just starting to scowl back when the woman's face lit up.

"Golden hair, golden eyes, and an impertinent, surly look. Would you by any chance be the little girl in Gareth's familia?"

"!"

Aiz's eyes opened in surprise.

"You know Gareth?"

"Of course. I've contracted with him. I see; I see. You're the Aiz Wallenstein he mentioned..."

After convincing herself of the young girl's identity, she offered her name.

"I go by Tsubaki. *Hephaistos Familia* blacksmith."

Aiz was stunned again at the name she spoke—not Tsubaki but that of the familia she belonged to.

"Oh, I've heard stories about you and your rampages, massacring a swarm of monsters. You're called the Doll Princess, aren't you? Ha-ha-ha, you are certainly as pretty as a doll, but—"

"Please!"

"Hmm?"

Aiz interjected as Tsubaki stroked her chin. She had a request for the bemused blacksmith.

"I'd like you to make a sword for me!"

Hephaistos Familia was the biggest blacksmithing group in the Labyrinth City at the moment. Their name was known around the world. Even someone as oblivious as Aiz recognized the Ἥφαιστος logo. If she could get a member of that famous smithing familia to make a sword for her, then...

Aiz looked at her with hopeful eyes.

"Hrmph..."

In response, Tsubaki squinted her right eye.

"Why do you want me to make you something?"

"Because I think you must be an amazing blacksmith...!"

"Why do you want a sword?"

"The swords I use...all break...so I want a sword that won't...!"

Aiz did not notice Tsubaki's gaze as she stumbled over her words, looking for how to respond.

Her gaze swept over the girl's body. Scrawny limbs, bruised skin, unkempt hair.

"If you got a sword, what would you do?"

"—I want to become strong."

Finally, her right eye met the dark flame in Aiz's grim, golden eyes.

After a moment's pause, Tsubaki smiled.

"I refuse."

When Aiz was visibly shocked, she elaborated.

"I have no intention of giving you a weapon."

"Why?!"

"I'm not interested."

"Wh—?"

"No, 'I can't stomach the thought' might be a better way to put it. Either way, give up. Craftsmen are the kind of people who won't budge if they're not interested. Myself included."

Aiz was about to argue more with Tsubaki, since she was being so vague about why she was turning down the request, but then the smith responded.

"Besides…'I want a sword that won't break'? What a strange thing to say."

Time froze when she heard the next words out of Tsubaki's mouth.

"If you want a *sword that's not broken yet*, there's one right there, isn't there?"

Tsubaki pointed straight at Aiz.

"Eh…"

The girl could not move.

Her outstretched finger was definitely pointing at Aiz.

What is she saying?

At the moment, Aiz was not even wearing a sword belt, let alone a sword.

A sword…Where…?

No.

What she is pointing at.

What she is looking at is—

—me?

The moment Aiz instinctively realized it, the woman narrowed her eyes and curled her lips. To Aiz in the moment, the smile looked like a mockery.

"Oh, the rain stopped."

Aiz was frozen stiff, but Tsubaki ignored her and cheered the rain passing.

"Well then, little girl. If you want a weapon, look elsewhere."

She parted with those words.

The wound remained in Aiz's heart, as if a sharpened blade had stabbed her.

A sword that hasn't broken yet?

A sword that will someday break?

Me...a sword...?

Even after Tsubaki left, Aiz could not move from that spot.

"Oh, ye finally came back!"

The sky was shrouded in darkness.

Gareth breathed a sigh of relief as he saw Aiz approaching the manor, hanging her head.

"Where'd you go, lass? I was just lookin' for you with Riveria."

"..."

"We were getting worried...Aiz?"

Noticing her unusual behavior, Gareth changed his tone as he called out to her. Her shoulders jumped. She lifted her face and finally noticed Gareth was there.

"Gar...eth..."

"Did something happen?"

"...I met a person with an eye patch...Tsubaki..."

"What? What about Tsubaki?"

Watching Aiz sluggishly nod, Gareth furrowed his brow as if sensing what had happened.

"Did she tell you something?"

"..."

He waited patiently without speaking, and finally the young girl explained in her small voice.

"She…I'm…a sword…"

"…"

"I'm a sword…That's what she said…"

Even as she was speaking, Aiz could not understand why she had been so stricken by it.

But that gaze and the smile she saw at the time were still etched into her brain. Those words had struck her at her core.

I'm a sword?

Not a person, a weapon?

A sword that would someday break? Destined to be destroyed?

All of a sudden, Aiz did not know what she was anymore. She lost sight of herself. Those simple words of Tsubaki's—the assessment she could not deny—had shaken her.

Her heart raced to an uneasy beat.

Aiz didn't want to look in a mirror. She was afraid she might not see herself in the reflection. She might see something else entirely.

"Oof, Tsubaki…Ye sure opened a big can of worms."

Seeing Aiz in this state, Gareth breathed his biggest sigh of the day. He had forged a direct contract with the smithing specialist and he knew her personality all too well, which was why he directed an extra-large complaint her way.

Gareth called out to the still-soaked girl.

"Aiz, after you warm up in the bath, come to my room."

"…Eh?"

"I'll talk to Riveria and Finn for you."

Gareth left Aiz with that as she looked up to see him lumbering back to the manor.

Aiz just stood there for a minute before slowly dragging herself to the bath to get rid of the chill like he suggested. After steadily warming herself up, she changed into the dressing gown that had been prepared for her at some point. She wandered hesitantly for a bit before heading to Gareth's room.

Her destination was directly beneath Finn's office, at the north end of the collection of spires that formed the manor.

"Aye, so ye came?"

Aiz thought the room was the exact opposite of Riveria's.

Axes and greatswords and other large weapons and shields were everywhere, giving it a vaguely rustic feel. In the corner was a sooty treasure chest that showed its age, drawing the eye. There was a large desk, shortened to suit a dwarf, and a collection of tools that appeared to be for tinkering with things was laid out across it. There was a large collection of documents as well, though not as many as Riveria had. Instead of magic-stone lamps, there was a lantern that looked like it burned coal.

In the middle of the room, Gareth was sitting on his bed. His ax, what looked like Aiz's shortsword, a hand towel and some wool, some knives and other tools were all spread across a sheet atop the bed as well.

"Gareth, that's..."

"Aye. I'm going to teach you how to maintain your weapons."

Aiz blinked over and over at his sudden declaration.

Not minding her reaction, Gareth beckoned to her. "Come on—over here."

Bewildered, Aiz did as he said and sat on the bed with him. She watched him as he sat at ease, rummaging through the sparkling tools before suddenly pushing her sword and a cloth into her hands.

"Try to do it just like I tell you. First, run it along the core of the blade..."

"L-like this?"

Following his instructions, she began the weapon's maintenance. Aiz grew flustered when she couldn't emulate Gareth's movements the way she intended; it forced her to acknowledge once again just how unskilled she was. Still, she did not have anything else to do at the moment, so she silently focused on her work.

After Gareth taught her what to do, he returned to wiping down his own weapon. When Aiz made a mistake or did not know what to do next, he would wrap his large hand around hers and tell her, "Like this," explaining it in a few words.

She had thought he always sounded so exciting, but the way he put his hands on hers was soft and kind.

It was difficult to describe the mood as the time passed. The dwarf fell silent as the two of them continued to polish their weapons together.

If she'd had a grandfather…it probably would have felt like this.

As something whispered in the recesses of her heart…

"Aiz, ye see…you have to take care of your weapons like this."

Gareth broke his silence.

"…?"

"If you leave them soaking in monster blood, they'll rust. If even a speck of dust sticks to them, the edges will grow dull. Weapons seem sturdy, but the reality is that they're delicate things."

"…"

"There's a saying. 'Weapons are an extension of their wielder.' We have to take care of them as parts of ourselves."

"That's…What?"

Without raising his face, still focused on his ax, Gareth narrowed his eyes.

"It's the same for adventurers."

"!"

Aiz opened her eyes wide at those words.

"Look at the sword in your hands. It's the weapon you were using today. It's covered in wounds…just like you right now."

"…!"

"That's what Tsubaki meant."

The rusted shortsword in her hands exemplified the truth that Aiz had refused to recognize.

Just like Gareth said, the sword was damaged all over. She looked at all the nicks left on it. This *extension* of Aiz was crying out in pain right now.

She saw her scrawny arms, scarred skin, and damaged hair reflected in the steel blade.

© Kiyotaka Haimura

"If you don't pay attention, it wears down, and wears down, and wears down…and in the end, it breaks. Gone too soon."

"Oh…"

"But if ye take proper care and maintain it…Look, just like you see before you. Damaged weapons can regain their luster."

With one hand, Gareth lightly picked up his ax, its maintenance complete.

Just as he'd said, the weapon glinted with a sturdy light despite some lingering scars.

"Breaking isn't the only fate swords can have. If you can bring back their shine like this, if you put together the broken pieces, they can be reborn, too."

"Gareth…"

"That's why you have to take care of your weapons—and of yourself, too. If you can do that, it will be your first step to becoming a fine adventurer."

Looking at Aiz, Gareth broke into a wrinkled smile.

With his compassionate expression buried in his beard, he seemed cheerful and kind, like a gentle old man.

His hand felt warm as he patted her head, tousling her hair.

For a second, Aiz thought she felt a tingling in the backs of her eyes, but she dismissed it as her imagination. There was no way that could be.

Aiz looked down at the sword in her hands and began polishing it again.

She restored the shine of her blade as Gareth looked on with a peaceful gaze.

From that day on, Aiz made a daily habit of taking care of her sword.

She would do it every night without fail in the room she had been given on the top floor of the spire, working by moonlight beside the window instead of turning on a lamp. Sitting atop her bed, she would trace over her damaged sword.

She had stopped saying she wanted strong weapons. She used the one Gareth had picked out for her like an extension of herself, carefully balancing her fiercer sword techniques and her more precise techniques in their due places. She stuck with it until it was time to part, and at that point, she felt like she had acquired something important.

She also started eating properly at breakfast, lunch, and dinner. She even managed to get the carrots she hated into her mouth with a straight face, with all the stiffness of a mannequin. Though she did wince once they were safely inside. The more senior members of the familia who she did not interact with much were shocked to see her in the dining hall and struggled to contain their laughter at her struggle against the carrots.

"Aiz."

"Riveria…"

"Could…That is, would…you let me help you take care of your hair?"

"…Okay."

And she also brushed her hair.

Riveria was surprised when Aiz nodded at her doubt-filled request, but finally she smiled and brought the girl to her own room to arrange her hair.

The first time, there was an awful lot of exchanges like "Owww!" and "J-just be patient!" but as the days passed, Riveria's care reached a level fit for a queen—elegant and gentle, reminiscent of a loving attendant.

She stood directly behind Aiz, who sat in a chair as the brush ran through her hair with soft sounds. Glancing at the full-length mirror, she noticed that Riveria's face looked gentler than she had ever seen it before.

"Hey…Riveria."

"What is it, Aiz?"

"Are you growing your hair out?"

"Hmm, yes. My hair has always grown quickly. When I explore the labyrinth, it gets in the way, so I usually cut it short whenever I come back to Orario, but…"

Kiyotaka Haimura

"...?"

"...Loki...said that it was better for someone in my position to let it grow out, so I decided to give it a try."

"In your position?"

"N-nothing for you to concern yourself with."

Riveria's jade hair extended down her back, held in place by a single hair band. She did not hesitate to say it was just a whim, but the reason she had picked that golden hair band was because of the golden-haired, golden-eyed girl.

Aiz was still far younger, but from behind, they looked almost like sisters, or perhaps a mother and daughter.

"..."

"..."

"..."

Hearing the sound of the brush through the cracked door, Finn, Gareth, and Loki peeked in so silently that even the high elf first-tier adventurer did not notice them. They exchanged smiles.

The prum leader nodded deeply, as if acknowledging something.

"Aiz, I'm going to have a weapon made for you."

This was the first thing Aiz heard after being called into the office.

At first she did not know how to respond and just stared in puzzlement.

"What's this? It's the custom weapon ye've been wanting, isn't it? You should be happier!"

"...Is it okay?"

"Yes. We all talked it over and agreed that now is the right time."

Aiz's gaze shifted from the smiling Gareth to Finn and then to Riveria standing next to them. The high elf smiled suddenly with closed eyes.

Setting Aiz aside, since she could not quite believe it was real yet, Loki started bubbling over in excitement.

"Awww right! Aizuu's first-ever made-to-order weapon! I'll take care of getting it made like I did with the armor. It's gonna be a suuuper-special blade!"

"It's a weapon for a lower-class adventurer. Don't get carried away."

As Loki excitedly fist-pumped, she was brought back down to Earth by a blow from Riveria's staff.

"Guooo?!"

Leaving their patron goddess rolling around on the ground, they split up.

However, as the days passed, Aiz couldn't deny the excitement growing in her.

She couldn't say whether it was anticipation or trepidation. Most likely, it was some of both.

Aiz went to see the craftsmen who had taken the order a few times, and then she spent several sleepless nights waiting for the day to come.

And so, one week after Finn's pronouncement...

"You're here, huh...?"

A stern-faced old god waited in the workshop beneath the three overlapping hammers of the faction's emblem that hung overhead.

Goibniu Familia. They were slightly less well known, but they were a solid smithing familia whose quality neither surpassed nor fell behind *Hephaistos Familia*'s.

According to Loki, "*The old man's curious about ya!*" so Aiz was a bit tense as she followed behind Goibniu.

Riveria and Gareth looked on as she took the item that was placed on the pedestal.

"Try drawing it."

"...Okay."

She drew the blade from its scabbard and held it in both hands, raising it up.

It was significantly longer than any sword she had used before. It was still in the shortsword category, but for Aiz's current size, it was effectively a longsword. The blade's body had a wave running through it, a line dividing the extra-hardened blade edge from the more flexible spine. She could tell even without testing it that it was incredibly sharp.

It was a beautiful sword with a pale tinge of blue to it. Riveria and Gareth were astonished, while Aiz had been left speechless and instantly in love.

"The sword's name is…Sword Air."

"Sword Air…"

The sword's name tumbled from her lips.

Raising her first trusted sword to the ceiling, Aiz saw Sword Air's blade shimmer.

CHAPTER
3

FROM THE NORTH MOUNTAINS

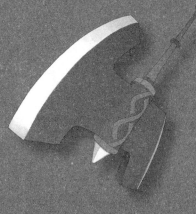

Гэта казка́ пачынае́цца сям...

Да поўначы ад гары

Well this is a problem… Aiz thought.

A fireplace crackled. The room's warmth penetrated the chill that had gotten into her bones from the rain. Aiz had stripped off her battle gear and underwear, leaving her naked as she wiped down her supple, smooth arms. She glanced to the side.

"Ah, you're really pretty, Miss Aiz…I'm sorry all I have to offer is my tacky clothes. I'll at least pick out the cutest outfit I have for you!"

Seeing Aiz's gorgeous figure, which most adventurers couldn't possibly ignore, the good-natured village girl enthusiastically prepared an armful of clothes. The way her eyes sparkled in excitement reminded Aiz of Lefiya, so Aiz could guess what was about to happen to her.

Though she was certainly somewhat concerned about being used as a doll for dress-up, the bigger issue was the situation they had landed in.

Rakia had somehow managed to kidnap a goddess.

Upon hearing the news, many gods and goddesses as well as representatives from various familias gathered at the north gate. Amid that confusion, Aiz had volunteered to rescue Hestia.

Bell from *Hestia Familia* had volunteered as well. Loki and Finn, who had taken over as commanders of the Orario forces, had approved it, so she and Bell formed an emergency two-man rescue party.

Directly after setting out from Orario, they caught up to the Rakian army in the Beor Mountain Range that lay due north of the city, but in the ensuing skirmish, the captive goddess, Hestia, had been knocked off a cliff into a valley. Bell jumped from the mountain path down the cliff face before anyone else could move and Aiz followed after—that was how disaster struck.

The Beor Mountain Range was a collection of peaks that formed a natural fortress. There were extant monster species that had first emerged back during the Ancient Times, and the Devil Mountains' extreme inclines and poor trails made it easy to get lost, even for an adventurer used to exploring the Dungeon. Heading out in the current torrential rain was simply asking for trouble.

In the midst of all that, the ones who lent them a helping hand were the residents of Edas Village.

"All right, perfect! You look way better than I ever did in it!"

"Thank you…"

Her time as the village girl's dress-up doll was shorter than expected. Aiz had donned a long red skirt with colorful embroidery, a white blouse, and a multicolored button-up vest. She looked like an average village girl, but it was much cuter than her standard adventurer's battle clothes and equipment. Plus, she wasn't used to dressing in this style of clothing. Aiz blushed ever so slightly. Rina, the human girl standing before her, broke into a smile.

After falling into the valley, they had been attacked by monsters. The residents of Edas Village had found them after hearing the cries of the monsters and guided them back to here. They were shown to the largest residence, which belonged to the village elder.

Rina was the elder's daughter.

"Oh, Miss Adventurer…Have you finished changing?"

"Yes. Thank you for everything."

After leaving Rina's room and going into the hallway, she ran into the village elder himself.

His name was Kam. With dull white hair and a small beard, he was well into his twilight years and walked with a cane. He was a human like his daughter, Rina, but he was paler. Aiz could tell he was afflicted by some kind of sickness.

She smiled pleasantly in her new outfit for the kind old man who was making such an effort to care for them despite his condition.

"It really suits you. You almost look like a goddess."

"…Thank you very much."

Blushing, Aiz could only repeat her thanks.

Kam smiled slightly, and he seemed almost nostalgic as he admired her long golden hair and beauty that could rival the gods themselves. Shaking his head slightly, he spoke again.

"The goddess...Lady Hestia's condition doesn't seem critical. Bell is in the inner room taking care of her."

"Okay..."

"I told Bell the same, but please make yourself at home here. If there are any problems, feel free to ask Rina or someone else. Ask for anything at all."

Rina smiled in agreement. Aiz lowered her head in thanks for their incredible hospitality.

"Ah...Aiz."

"Everything okay?"

"Fine. She's just sleeping now..."

Hestia was sleeping on the bed and Bell sat right beside her, watching over her rest as a fire crackled in the hearth. Aiz had actually been asking about Bell, who was clearly worn out, but all he could think of at the moment was Hestia.

Unlike the two adventurers, Hestia was as weak as the average person when her Arcanum was sealed. Thanks to Bell shielding her, she wasn't terribly injured, but in addition to falling into the valley, she had been drenched in the downpour.

Mm-hmm...This is...problematic.

Until Hestia recovered, they couldn't leave this village.

Even though they had been in an accident, it wouldn't be that difficult for Aiz to return to Orario by herself. All she had to do was head for a place where she could get a clear view, then set a course to the city. Even if she had to blaze her own path, she could make it down the mountain without issue. However, the Rakians were still in the area.

They wouldn't stop Aiz, but they had more than enough to surround and defeat a second-tier adventurer like Bell. If Hestia was kidnapped again while Aiz was busy getting help from Orario, she wouldn't be able to live with herself.

After they'd carried Hestia to this residence, Aiz had gone out again searching for the path they had fought on earlier, but she couldn't find a trace of the enemy. It was hard to imagine they had noticed Edas Village, at least...But the best option was for all three of them to move together. After talking it over with Bell earlier, she had agreed to this plan.

"Aiz, I'm really sorry...for causing so much trouble."

"It's fine...Besides...it's not your fault."

This was the third time Bell had apologized for getting her involved, but she only shook her head.

He looked up apologetically and reacted with surprise when he finally noticed her village-girl outfit. Then, as if realizing he was blushing, he quickly turned away.

Aiz tilted her head in confusion, not sure why he was the one getting embarrassed. Eventually, she peered out the window

The rain was still pouring in the dark night.

Are Tione, Tiona, and Lefiya worried...? It's probably a problem for Finn and Loki, too...

Their familia was trying to deal with the Evils that were rearing their head. This wasn't the time for one of the core members of *Loki Familia* to be somewhere far away from Orario, but...

Aiz imagined her comrades' faces as she said a silent apology to each of them, with the high elf last of all.

Riveria...will probably get mad at me.

Outside the city—far from her home—that thought suddenly came to mind.

Along with it was the unfamiliar feeling of a child being scolded by her mother for coming home late.

Harsh weather persistently hung over the Beor Mountain Range.

It was their second day staying in the village. Aiz watched the rain continue to fall from the windowsill.

Another search-and-rescue squad would probably be forming up in Orario around now. But in this weather, the risk of another accident was high, so they wouldn't range out too far afield looking for them.

Because of the rain, Aiz couldn't leave the house, either. She was disappointed she couldn't do her daily practice, but she couldn't bring herself to swing a sword inside a house they were borrowing.

Looking around, she could see a few people out walking around in rain gear. They seemed to be preparing for something, carrying what looked to be ritual tools.

"I'm sorry for asking you to help me with the chores."

"No problem…You're letting us stay here, after all."

Aiz snapped back to her senses as the girl next to her spoke up.

Rina was smiling as she shook her black hair back and forth. Aiz was standing in the washing area.

Unlike Orario, this village far up in the mountains didn't have magic-stone technology everywhere. Apparently, they usually pulled water from a nearby spring, but at the moment, they were using a bucket filled with rainwater.

"I'd heard stories before, but adventurers from Orario are really amazing. Falling into the valley without getting hurt and even clearing out a horde of monsters, all without breaking a sweat."

"Hmm? I guess I'm used to it?"

"Ah-ha-ha. So I guess there are a lot of adventurers like you in Orario."

"Have you ever been…?"

"I've never gone. I haven't left the village much. I'm interested, but I have to take care of my dad."

Rina was a good-natured, caring girl. A total sweetheart.

Aiz thought she was far more attractive than herself, a woman of few words and muted expression.

From listening to her talk, she gathered they were around the same age. However, despite being her father, Kam was old enough to be her grandfather. Aiz was curious about that, but she kept it to herself.

"Has this village always been here?"

"Yes. They say its history goes back to the Ancient Times. It used to be an elf village."

Aiz was surprised to hear that, but it made sense. Deep inside the harsh mountaintops, surrounded by precipitous rock faces, this was the perfect place for a hidden settlement.

Edas Village was apparently a gathering of people who had abandoned the world.

Humans who had fallen into despair at their situation and demi-humans who had gotten into trouble, people who had fallen in love with someone from another race—anyone who had lost their place in the world. The residents of this village had welcomed those who wandered into the Beor Mountain Range since long ago. There were even some stray adventurers who had been chased out of Orario. More than half the villagers were descendants of those wanderers for one reason or another. Because of their background, they were tolerant of outsiders and people who had run into trouble like Aiz's group.

It wasn't marked on any map, a village for drifters who had nowhere else to go.

A world I didn't know existed...

For Aiz, who had spent all her time swinging her sword deep in Orario's Dungeon, it was a world she had never encountered before. Aiz was woefully ignorant and inexperienced with anything that didn't relate directly to fighting and the Dungeon. That was exactly why Riveria and the others had tried to expose her to various different things when she was younger.

There was one time Riveria had invited her out.

"Why don't you try traveling outside Orario once?"

At the time, Aiz was desperate to obtain more power as soon as possible, so she had refused the offer, but she thought she understood now what Riveria had wanted to convey to her.

She didn't know anything. About this Earth—about the world as it was now.

"Thank you very much. That's everything."

"If you need help with anything else…"

"In that case, could you go check on the goddess for me? With this rain, there are so many things I have to get done…"

Rina looked a little embarrassed as she accepted Aiz's offer to continue helping.

With a fresh towel and a bucket of water, Aiz headed to the room where Hestia was resting.

"Ah…I'm sorry for asking you to get supplies."

"No need…Here."

Bell turned around when Aiz entered the room. He was still sitting in the chair next to the bed like he had been the day before.

After exchanging a couple of words with him, she handed over the simple bucket. The boy wet a towel in the water and wrung it out before replacing the cloth lying across the goddess's forehead. He also refilled the water pitcher absentmindedly. Aiz couldn't exactly take care of a different familia's patron deity, so she simply watched, leaving it to the goddess's follower. Bell's motions seemed well practiced.

It was like she was peeking into the very beginnings of the tiny familia that had consisted of just the two of them until recently. Or perhaps it was simply his upbringing. Either way, Aiz felt like she was getting a glimpse of another side of him she hadn't seen before. He had probably tended to someone before Hestia, perhaps a family member.

"Uuunnn…"

"Ah. Goddess. Are you okay? Do you need anything?"

At that point, Hestia's eyes opened.

As Bell leaned in, she said, "I'm fine, thank you…" before turning her blue-tinted eyes toward Aiz.

"I'm sorry, Wallensomething…I caused…you a lot of trouble."

"No…"

"Also…thank you. For helping Bell…and me."

The goddess offered a sincere apology and gratitude. Though she was still suffering from a fever, she managed to smile.

Aiz felt like whenever they met, Hestia was always giving her warnings or advice, but the goddess had a genuine divinity about her, too. She and that simple boy made a good familia.

"I'm sorry, Bell...Is it okay if I go back to sleep?"

"Yes, of course. Take your time and rest."

Hestia lowered her eyes apologetically, her voice tinged with fatigue. Bell nodded kindly and adjusted her blanket.

Watching him provide such tender care and attention, Aiz suddenly thought of Riveria.

She couldn't remember anymore, but they had probably played out this scenario themselves.

"She's...much better..."

"Yes...Thanks to Kam and the others...and you."

There was an empty plate atop a small table in the room. Hestia had eaten the porridge set out this morning, apparently. Her voice had regained much of its strength as well. She wasn't fully recovered, but her condition had improved greatly after a day's rest.

Hestia was lightly sweating, but Aiz decided it would be better for her or Rina to towel her off later. She shifted her gaze to Bell.

"Did you...get any rest?"

He was still in the exact same spot as the day before, continuing to take care of the goddess.

Bell had scarcely left the room. The boy didn't appear too tired on the outside, but she could tell that he had stayed up all night.

"It's nothing. I may look like a mess, but I am a Level Three, after all."

It was true that adventurers who had leveled up were significantly tougher than the average person. It might have been a different story in the Dungeon, where just standing inside could be draining, but one or two all-nighters here wouldn't be the end of the world...But that was no excuse to force things, either.

As Bell tried to laugh it off, Aiz countered quietly.

"You need to rest. You were...running around the mountain yesterday."

"..."

"Hestia...wouldn't want this, either...I think."

Gnawing her lip as she struggled to find the words, Aiz somehow managed to speak her thoughts. She spoke quietly so that their conversation wouldn't find its way into the goddess's dreams.

Bell's smile withered, and he looked down.

"But it's my fault...I caused so many problems for the goddess and you..."

He closed his rubellite eyes once, then shifted his gaze to the goddess as his sentence trailed off. Aiz thought that Bell's kindness and modesty were virtues, but they were also a source of his painful tendency to be self-deprecating. She had already told him last night that none of this was his fault, but he still blamed himself.

"All this happened because the goddess and I got into a fight...If it wasn't for that, she wouldn't have gotten kidnapped..."

The boy had suddenly taken things in a totally unexpected direction.

"A fight...? You...and Hestia?"

"Ah, no...Not really a fight per se, but...Anyway, it's complicated..."

Aiz was genuinely surprised as he struggled to correct himself before trailing off into silence once more. She couldn't imagine the gentle boy before her getting into a fight with anyone, let alone his goddess. Even Aiz, who was generally blind to people's unspoken thoughts, could tell that something had happened.

As she stared at him, Bell looked even more uncomfortable than before. Making up her mind, she pulled a chair next to the boy and sat down.

"A-Aiz...?"

"..."

"Uh, um..."

"...Talk."

"Eh?"

"Let's...talk."

Bell was startled as Aiz struggled to convey her intent despite her clumsy command of language.

"If something is bothering you…I'll listen…"

In the end, she finally initiated conversation with Bell. Normally, Aiz wouldn't have been able to bring herself to do it, but perhaps she managed this time because she had remembered how she had been in the past. She wanted to try to guide him like Riveria, Gareth, and Finn had guided her. At the very least, he was a student she had schooled in her fighting style.

And even if she believed she wasn't cute at all, she was still a woman like Hestia. She should have a way to help him somehow. The young Aiz in her heart had suddenly grown eager, like she was sliding on a pair of glasses to show she was getting serious.

Doing her best to hide those feelings, she tried to look attentive—but Bell seemed uneasy and hesitant to respond.

"No, um…About what happened, I don't really want to talk… about it…Um…"

Aiz felt a little bit offended.

It was obviously hard to say, or at least hard to bring up in discussion. But when she saw his eyes darting back and forth, she sensed something else. *The topic is difficult and delicate, so talking about it with you isn't exactly…*was the feeling she got from him. There was no way to know, but she suspected if one of the gods was here instead of her, Bell would probably talk about it.

—*That means I'm not good enough!*

Aiz's self-esteem took a bit of a beating.

In fact, the boy in front of her was the one person she didn't want to treat her that way. Aiz couldn't stand it. She wanted to seem more reliable to him. Perhaps it was because she was older than he was. The bespectacled little girl in her heart was yelling and waving both arms.

Her doll-like face donned a stubborn expression.

"…Bell."

"Y-yes?"

"I taught you how to fight."

"Y-yes."

"That means…I'm…like……your master."

Brushing away the intense feelings of hesitation and embarrassment, Aiz somehow managed to put her thoughts into words.

She understood better than anyone that she wasn't really suited to being a teacher, but just this one time, with this one boy, she wanted to wear that mantle. She wanted to be what her teachers had been for her.

Memories of Riveria, Finn, and Gareth all trying to persuade her crossed her mind.

As her cheeks grew a bit hotter, Aiz tried her best to speak with authority.

However.

"Master...?"

The boy looked like he had laid eyes on something impossible to even fathom.

Her cheeks twitched, and Aiz—*snapped.*

"...What?"

"Ah...N-nothing..."

"If you have something you want to say...say it."

"A-are you...mad—?"

"I'm not mad."

That was a lie.

She was furious.

She had not noticed that her eyebrows were scrunched up and her cheeks were on the verge of puffing into a grumpy pout.

Getting out of her seat, she approached Bell.

"Talk to me."

"Eh, um, but...?!"

"Talk to me."

"I...I can't!"

"Why?"

"There's no way I can when you're like this!"

A dangerous blaze was growing behind her golden eyes as Bell finally shouted.

This little—What a terrible student!

At that point, Aiz finally had a small taste of Riveria's past struggle. She felt like she could sympathize with the elf from nine years ago.

Is this what it's like trying to teach a problem child?!

"Talk to me."

"Aiz! Aiz?!"

"Talk to me."

"Too close, too close, too close!"

"Talk. To. Me."

"S-someone?! Help me!!!"

Turning red, Bell desperately pleaded for help as Aiz moved close enough for their noses to touch.

Aiz quickly grabbed his shoulders. There was no escaping the first-tier adventurer.

Bell could hold out no longer and blushed a beet red.

"Ugh, you're so loud—Wait, what are you doing?!!!!!"

As Hestia struggled to open her eyes, she screamed when she saw the assault unfolding before her.

"Wh-what are you guys doing?! Wallensomething! Get away from Beeell!!"

Seeing their faces that close, Hestia instantly assumed they were about to kiss. She was like a wife who had caught her husband cheating on her.

The agitated goddess tried to jump out of bed, momentarily forgetting all about recovering from her sickness.

But as Bell desperately tried to resist, he turned his body awkwardly, and his foot slipped.

""Oh.""

Aiz and Bell spoke at the same time. As Hestia tried to leap out of bed, it looked like Aiz was trying to push Bell down, and the pair tumbled into the goddess.

"Guaaaaaaaaaaaaaaaaaaa?!"

"G-Goddessssssss?!"

Bell and Aiz's scuffle landed a blow right to Hestia's gut.

The goddess's scream echoed through the village elder's home.

"Bell, Aiz…Please try to treat the goddess with a little more care…"

Kam spoke their names gravely before giving his request rather awkwardly.

The two shrank back, ashamed of themselves.

It was time for dinner. After what had happened earlier, the pair headed to the dining room. If they stayed in the room with the goddess, it wouldn't have been good for her peace of mind.

At first, a near-crazed Hestia had been screaming, "Bring me Wallensomething!" but naturally, it was impossible for her to maintain that level of energy, and she eventually wore herself out. Still panting from the effort, she obediently slipped back into bed, exhausted.

"Dad, they seem like they're sorry already, so that's enough. Let's have dinner."

They began eating supper at Rina's suggestion. Foraged plants from the mountain and fish caught from the river made up most of the food.

There were seven people around the table, including Aiz and Bell and Kam and Rina. Besides Rina, Kam had three sons who lived at the residence. They were all older than her and all half-breeds, crosses with elves and animal people.

They were as polite and cheerful as Rina, so warm conversation developed around the table.

"Aiz, about earlier…"

Sitting to her left, Bell trembled as he looked like he was about to apologize, but Aiz was being difficult and looked away from him in a pout. Complete despair crossed his face. Watching the two of them, Rina and Kam chuckled.

"I thought you looked like a doll at first, but…Bell can get that expression out of you."

"…?"

Across from Aiz, sitting next to Kam, Rina smiled.

What expression? Aiz just cocked her head in confusion, not sure what the girl was trying to say.

Hanging his head from the shock, Bell didn't register what she had said at all.

"How about one drink, Bell? I brought some special alcohol from the storehouse that's just right for occasions like this."

"Ah…Um, I'm not really one for—"

"Come on, brother. Can't you see Bell's uncomfortable?"

The animal person sitting to Aiz's right had been offering the wooden mug of alcohol he had poured for Bell. He just shrugged and looked wistfully at the untouched drink, then set it back in front of himself when Rina scolded him…

Watching the back-and-forth going on around her, Aiz glanced at the boy.

*What should I do? I was probably being immature, and I want to make up with him, but I'm still kind of mad at him…*She cycled through those thoughts in her mind. The young Aiz in her heart raged like a minotaur.

She knew that Bell was discreetly peeking over at her, too. Feeling extremely awkward as her mind raced over what to do, she reached out for the mug next to her.

The one she picked up wasn't hers, though. It was the one set aside by Kam's son.

And the second it touched her lips—

—Aiz blacked out.

Immediately after that—*splash!*

"Hgn?"

She was confused as she felt water hitting her face.

Unsure what had just happened, Aiz realized that her face and clothes were drenched and finally together that someone had thrown a lot of water at her. Rina was standing in front of her, shoulders heaving as she took ragged breaths, an empty pail in her hands.

...I was splashed with water? Why?

She was still confused about that point, but that doubt changed into shock.

"Wh...? Bell?!"

For some reason, the boy had been beaten half to death and was collapsed on the floor, barely breathing.

Not just Bell. The table and chairs had been strewn around the room to create a spectacular mess. It looked like a storm had torn through. Aiz was totally confused.

What the hell?

It was just a second!

What happened?!

Kam's sons were pale, standing up against the wall holding the plates of food. Kam himself was sitting on the floor with his mouth half-open. It almost looked like his spirit was about to escape through his mouth and seek refuge in heaven as one of his sons approached him, crying, "Dad! Daaaaaaad?!" It was a catastrophe.

Could it be...?

"An enemy attack?!"

I didn't sense...anything...But that's impossible!

Aiz shuddered as she immediately prepared herself. For some reason, there was a bloody wooden club in her right hand, so she readied it, constantly wheeling around looking for the assailant.

"A-Aiz...Agh."

Bell managed to squeeze out a few syllables, sounding like a rabbit squashed at Aiz's feet. She looked deadly serious as a bead of sweat dripped down her cheek. His right hand was clinging to a jet-black knife. He had clearly struggled valiantly against the attacker. However, the enemy had shown no hesitation in beating him black and blue.

The callous brutality of it enraged Aiz.

The assailant was someone who could do all that to a second-tier adventurer like Bell...!

Her caution level skyrocketed. For some reason, the enemy hadn't attacked her, perhaps out of fear, but she couldn't let her guard down. Her piercing gaze patrolled the painfully silent dining room.

Because she was busy standing guard for potential enemies, she didn't realize.

The contents of the wooden mug had spilled across the floor in the chaos. The smell rising from the mug she had mistakenly sipped from was the scent of alcohol.

She didn't notice that the people trembling around the room were all staring at her.

"...Miss Aiz, please look after Mr. Bell."

"But the enemy...!"

Rina's shoulders heaved as if a sudden wave of exhaustion had hit her.

Glancing pitifully at Bell, she limply shook her head.

"No, it's fine. Also, I'm begging you—please don't do anything weird. In particular, please don't touch the alcohol spilled on the floor."

"But—"

"*I. Said. It. Is. Fine.*"

"O-okay."

Aiz tried to persist, but the pressure of Rina's intense gaze convinced Aiz to back down. She nodded her assent.

Rina and the boys looked like they had witnessed a tragedy as they started cleaning up. Aiz felt uneasy, but the attackers she was wary of never appeared. Kam gasped as he opened his eyes, so it all ended without incident.

For some reason, Aiz started feeling embarrassed, so she did as she was told and tended to Bell. Seeing his current state, her childish irritation was barely worth considering. It was all water under the bridge now. After treating his wounds with a potion, she felt lonely for some reason, so she rested his head on her lap.

She stroked his white hair.

She wasn't sure what the cause was, but all Bell could manage now was to groan in pain.

There might be an enemy we can't see...I have to protect Bell and the others!

Tightening her grip on the wooden bludgeon, she was brimming with resolve.

From that day onward, even after the rain stopped, she didn't take a single step outside the house, focusing solely on protecting them.

And Rina and her family, for some reason, wouldn't let Aiz anywhere near any alcoholic drinks.

GODS
AND
PEOPLE
FROM
DAYS
GONE PAST

Гэта казка іншага свя .

Мінулыя дні ад багі і людзі

Aiz entered *Loki Familia* during Orario's Dark Ages.

It could all be traced back to the fall of the two familias hailed as the strongest and their failure to fulfill the world's wish to complete the Three Great Quests. The latent evil in Orario reared its head and destroyed the public order of the city that lay at the center of the world.

Amid all that, the most powerful group was the Evils.

"Fu-ha-ha-ha! Do it! Sink the city into chaos!"

Even in broad daylight, the sounds of explosions and wails of grief joined one man's raucous laughter.

Standing on the roof of a half-destroyed building, a human man looked down at the struggle unfolding before his eyes. Known as Vendetta, one of the leaders of the Evils with a bounty on his head, Olivas Act howled with delight.

"Tch, Olivas, you bastard. You sure started it off with a bang...Oi! We aren't gonna lose to those shitheads! Don't let them get ahead of us!"

Seeing smoke rising in the distance, another leader of the Evils, known to some as Arachnia and to others as Valletta Grede, scoffed in annoyance as a lurid grin appeared on her face. She had been entrusted with leading an attack on the home of a familia supporting the Guild as well as aiming to steal supplies from the corporation, and she laughed in ecstasy as smoke and flames rose in the skies while the screams of fleeing residents and blades clashing to create sprays of blood and sparks wove together into a music to accompany the sight.

"All right! Bring it, you Guild dogs! Get out here, Fiiinnnnn! We're gonna have a fuuun party today, too!"

That was what Orario was like back then.

Pure chaos where public order was all but broken, where the battle between good and evil adventurers continued day in and day out.

"Everyone gather up at the front gate! Split into three groups around Riveria, Gareth, and me!"

Finn's orders flew as the manor filled with the sound of footsteps. As everyone started rushing around, Aiz ran to Finn.

"I'm going...too!"

"Absolutely not. You stay here. It's too soon for you to come."

Riveria firmly rejected Aiz's request.

The familia was headed into a fight against people. There was a chance they would have to kill someone. The little girl didn't need to experience this sort of battlefield yet, and they had no intention of bringing her with them.

Eight months after she'd joined, Aiz was told that she wouldn't be part of the combat unit and should remain on alert with the reserves at the manor.

"We'll finish this in a flash and be back before you know it. Take it easy."

"Okay, Loki, I'm leaving the rest to you."

"Mm-hmm, see ya later. Do your best."

Leaving Loki in charge, they headed out.

"Well then, seems like they've gone out. Whatcha doin', Aizuu? Wanna try acting your age a bit and play doctor together?! Heh-heh."

"...Practice swings...in the courtyard."

"Bah, no way!"

"Also...don't call me weird names."

Even though she was showing more emotion when she was around Finn and the others—particularly Riveria—she was still usually stiff and doll-like. She curtly turned her back on the perverted goddess.

However, Loki could see through her.

Aiz herself didn't fully realize how much she was feeling alienated and separated from everyone else. The dissatisfaction and loneliness of a withdrawn child was housed in those small hunched shoulders.

The next day.

Aiz was swinging her sword in the central yard again.

Her trusted Sword Air cut the air beneath blue sky that afternoon.

The custom sword that *Goibniu Familia* had made for her fit her hands perfectly. The weapon was made of Damascus, imported from outside the city. As its other moniker "rippled steel" implied, there was a light wave or ripple visible on the sword's blade. Harder than normal steel, the tough blade had not chipped once despite cutting down countless monsters. It had a bit of heft to it, and that force let it pierce through even an adventurer's heavy armor with ease. To avoid being thrown off-balance by the momentum of the heavier sword, she constantly practiced swinging.

The people driving back the Evils attack hadn't returned yet, so instead of the practice fights she had planned, she was crossing blades with an imaginary opponent. As if trying to brush aside idle thoughts, she unleashed her sword techniques into the void.

"…"

Loki had come into the courtyard and was watching her from the shade of a tree.

The sharp attacks were at odds with the young girl's appearance, but the sword's melody was beautiful.

The crisp techniques were another reason behind all the talk about the Doll Princess. She was still unpolished, but from time to time, the golden-eyed, golden-haired girl would display a technique that would catch the attention of even the elites.

"…Loki?"

Aiz finally noticed the goddess as she stopped swinging, breathing heavily after her stamina had given out.

Watching with a serious look on her face, Loki finally smiled and said, "Nice work!" as she handed Aiz a towel. "Hey, Aiz, did anyone ever teach ya how to use a sword?"

"…?"

"Finn and the others were talking about how good you are. From time to time, you do things they've never seen before, and ya don't even have a teacher."

"Huh...?"

"Same goes for me. Just now I couldn't take my eyes off ya."

Aiz looked down at her sword and her hands as Loki smiled and praised her.

She had gotten here just by frantically pushing forward, so she hadn't been aware of it. Techniques that could astonish Finn and Gareth, who were training her in the fundamentals...Did she really have something like that?

The gallant image of her father who she looked up to crossed her mind. A lone swordsman who silently swung his sword like Aiz was doing now. The hero Aiz had dreamed of when she was younger.

"It sounds like they've nipped the incident in the bud. There's some cleanup left, but Riveria and the others should be back in the evening."

As Aiz sank into thought, Loki shared the news she had come to say, smiling in satisfaction.

"It's nice they're all safe."

"...Not like I was worried."

"Oh? Are ya sulkin' 'cause ya didn't get invited?"

"Of course...not."

Aiz turned away in a huff at Loki's teasing.

Loki smiled wanly. Aiz had been angry since yesterday. As the girl got ready to start training again, the goddess attempted to smooth her feathers a little.

"Aizuu, how 'bout a change'a pace? Let's head out for a bit."

Aiz sheathed Sword Air in a scabbard strapped to her back.

Since she was still so small, if she hung the sword at her waist, it would drag along the ground, so she wore a sword belt diagonally over her shoulder. After Aiz had finished getting ready for her guard duty, Loki absentmindedly said, "All right, shall we?"

"Why are you...taking me with you?"

"Mm, because if I left ya alone, you'd just keep fightin'. If someone didn't force you, ya might go your whole life without takin' a break."

"I'm taking breaks...when Riveria and the others tell me to."

Aiz also told her again not to call her weird names, but Loki paid her no mind as she continued.

"We're headed for a place on East Main Street eventually, but let's just wander a bit first."

They walked along countless small side streets instead of the main thoroughfare, following the whims of a goddess with no sense of planning. No matter how annoyed Aiz got, Loki wouldn't stop calling her "Aizuu," so she finally gave up.

They were on a city street totally different from the Adventurers Way she often went to. Fruits and sundries were being sold on the corners as horse-drawn carts slowly rolled along. But what surprised Aiz most of all were the demolished buildings and damaged roads they walked past.

Aiz had never really understood what was happening in Orario. Once she had been allowed to go Dungeon crawling, she had not really ventured much beyond the manor, Babel, and Central Park connecting the two. Because she spent time only in the Dungeon and the manor, she had no way to really grasp how the city was faring. However, by taking a different path like this, she could understand just by looking around. There was a darkness clouding people's faces.

"There was an incident yesterday, after all. So the children are scared something else might happen."

Like Loki said, in addition to the tension among the residents, there were Guild members and adventurers out patrolling. There was a red-haired girl wearing an emblem with a sword and wings alongside a masked adventurer; an old god was somewhat overbearingly handing out items and saying, "I'll give ya potions!" and a graceful long-haired god was taking care of injured people along with his followers. They passed an array of people from all races and walks of life.

Looking around, Aiz realized that all of this was brought on by the sudden clashes and confrontations—by the emergence of evil.

This was the doing of the Evils who Riveria, Finn, and Gareth were fighting.

According to Loki, lots of people were considering leaving Orario because of the crisis.

"Why are people…fighting each other?"

Loki didn't respond immediately to Aiz's whispered question.

After putting her hands behind her head and looking up at the blue sky, she responded.

"It's got a lot to do with us gods, too, but…it's also just in the nature of children."

"Nature…?"

"Creation and destruction, order and chaos. Violence is just one side of children that can't be denied."

"…"

Aiz remained silent. Was her desire to fight not also part of that? Didn't they come from the same root?

"But even so, everyone wants a brighter tomorrow. They do all they can to make it happen."

"…?"

"For example, look over there."

Loki pointed to a single food stall.

The smell of savory potatoes wafted from the stall as the girl working it cut and prepared the food. JYAGA MARU KUN was written in Koine on the sign.

"'Let everyone have delicious food so that they can smile! The bundle of joy that makes every mouth in the city water, Jyaga Maru Kun!'…was how that jingle went, I think."

"Jyaga Maru Kun…?"

"Apparently, it just started up recently. You don't know about it, right, Aizuu? Let's have a bit," she said as she led Aiz to the stall.

After Loki put in her order, two servings came out in short order. Loki handed over a gold coin and took the two sets of potatoes with a smile and a "thanks." Aiz looked in wonder at the one she was handed.

It was some kind of flattened potato snack that had been coated in breading and fried. Because it was freshly made, the outside was piping hot, and the scent of potato mixed with oil reached Aiz's nose.

Staring intently at the food in her hands, she bit into it with a *crunch*.

"—!!"

The next instant, the flavor hit.

The taste of the oil and potato spread through her mouth. Opening her eyes in shock, Aiz was instantly won over.

That was Aiz's introduction to Jyaga Maru Kun.

"You like it, Aizuu…?"

Before she realized it, Loki had to buy a third Jyaga Maru Kun for her.

She grabbed the wrapper with both hands and chowed down wholeheartedly. But her mouth was so small that she looked like a squirrel as she nibbled at it.

Loki bought one last puff to eat as they walked into Central Park.

Aiz always cut through here, so she knew the path well. Finishing up her potato puff, Aiz looked around the familiar scenery when—

"—I am Ganeeeeeeeeeeeeeesha!!!"

"?!"

A mind-bogglingly loud voice reverberated in the air.

Aiz wildly looked around as the voice shattered the peaceful afternoon calm. She noticed a crowd on the east side of the plaza. The throng of people surrounded a vehicle much larger than a carriage, and standing atop it was an suspicious-looking elephant-faced god striking a pose. However, mysteriously, when the lavishly decorated vehicle approached with him atop it, the crowd broke into cheers.

Aiz was the one who ended up acting suspiciously in her confusion.

"Ganesha, you idiot…Buyin' a damn float in order to cheer up the scared kids? How much did that thing cost?! He's some special kinda stupid," Loki whispered to herself, watching his followers pull the float with tears streaming down their faces, forcing themselves to smile and think about the long-term view. Their familia's savings? It was hard to imagine they had enough cash on hand to cover something like that.

"What…is that? A monster…?"

Aiz's confusion was understandable, but Loki desperately tried to calm her down nonetheless, since she was about to draw her sword. The girl was clearly confused by the bizarre scene playing out in front of her.

The float with the god atop it was pivoting around Babel as it traversed the plaza. The crowd and commotion gradually arrived at Loki and Aiz, who was still unable to escape her confusion.

"—I! Am! Ganeshaaaaaa!!!—Hmm?!"

The twenty-seventh time he introduced himself, the elephant god noticed them and leaped out.

"Hup!"

"?!"

The odd god—er, Ganesha—landed in front of the pair as the crowd cheered.

"Loki! Good work yesterday! I was delighted by the results! Allow me to thank you!"

"Don't tell me that—tell Finn and the others. And yer too excitable, so go someplace else. Yer scarin' Aizuu."

"Ohhh. You're the rumored Doll Princess, huh?!"

The overly excited god looked down at her.

He was swarthy and muscle-bound, wearing his trademark elephant mask on his face. Aiz was petrified as the hot-blooded god gave her a thumbs-up and smiled.

"I am Ganesha! Nice to meet you!"

"…"

Without waiting for Aiz to respond, he hopped back atop the float with a "hup."

Ganesha and his companions started heading toward the Pleasure District like a passing storm, leaving Aiz without a clue as to what had just happened.

"Aizuuuu, let's go now."

"Ah…O-okay."

Snapping out of it, the pair started to move through Central Park, when—

"Oh? Isn't that Loki?"

"So it is. Long time no see."

"Oh? Fei-Fei! And Demeter!"

They ran into two goddesses who had just left Babel.

Of course, it was Aiz's first time meeting them. One had crimson hair; the other had bouncy honey-colored hair. The former had an eye patch over her right eye, while the latter's distinguishing characteristic was her shockingly well-endowed bosom.

"What are y'all doing?"

"I'm headed back to my shop. Demeter's distributing food."

"Hey, Loki, is that child there part of your familia?"

"Sure is. Allow me to introduce ya! This here's Aizuu, our new member! She's a super rookie with a bright future ahead of her! Aizuu, this is Fei-Fei and Demeter!"

"Come on—at least tell her my actual name," the crimson-haired, crimson-eyed goddess complained as she looked down at Aiz. "You're Aiz Wallenstein, right?…I heard about you from Tsubaki."

"…! Tsubaki? That…"

"Yes, Tsubaki Collbrande is one of my followers. I'm Hephaistos. Pleasure to meet you."

On hearing Hephaistos's name, Aiz felt embarrassed. She didn't expect this to be Tsubaki's patron goddess. She had thought the eye patch looked vaguely familiar. Sort of like children taking after their parents, she guessed.

"It sounded like she meddled in your business a bit, so I should apologize," Hephaistos said as she held out her hand. Aiz hesitated for a second before nervously reaching out with her own.

"Aiz Wallenstein…the Doll Princess? You're…"

Demeter looked closer, seemingly having heard of Aiz's exploits as an adventurer.

The goddess crouched down and looked at her for a little bit.

Aiz started to get confused when all of a sudden—*fwap*—Demeter wrapped her in a hug.

"?!"

"Awww, so cuuute~! She's much prettier than any doll!"

"Ah, yeah...D-Demeter? Aizuu's gonna suffocate, so maybe... Wait, *my* energy's really fadin' fast. At this rate, I'm gonna die...!"

Caught between those giant breasts, Aiz was bewildered. The picture they painted together was too much for Loki, sending her staggering back with blood trickling from her mouth and leaving her unable to intervene effectively. Hephaistos just smiled wryly.

Unable to escape those mountains despite her best efforts, Aiz could only be confused.

"I'll bring you the next batch of vegetables and fruits, Loki. As thanks for always protecting the city."

"Oh really? Thanks! But Aizuu doesn't really like a lot of vegetables."

"If you don't eat everything, you won't get bigger, you know?"

"~~~~~?!"

Aiz wasn't in a position to think about vegetables she didn't like, since she was being smothered by Demeter's bosom while the goddesses chatted.

Gods are mysterious beings.

Aiz's nostrils filled with a somewhat nostalgic smell. Because of that, she couldn't put up much resistance.

So many gods she didn't know. Weird, strange, pretty, affectionate. There was a myriad of deusdea.

And they were all gathered here, in Orario, the center of the world.

Aiz learned that by experiencing it firsthand.

"Huh...Is that the new girl at Loki's place?"

There was a golden-haired, golden-eyed girl playing with some goddesses.

A silver-haired goddess looked down on them from the highest floor of the giant white tower as she elegantly raised a glass of wine to her lips.

"A blindingly golden spirit…and also incredibly sharp. Almost like a blade. She's the first I've seen who shines like that."

The lovely deity, who boasted a beauty unmatched by anyone, was sporting a smile that could charm anyone who caught a glimpse of it. A smile of deep interest.

However, the vermilion-haired goddess peered up as if she had noticed her gaze.

The bright color of her hair matched the narrow slits of her eyes—she was warning the bewitching deity that she knew what was going on.

If ya try anything funny, ya won't get away with it.

"I won't steal her."

The silver-haired goddess shrugged and smiled again in response to the goddess she had known for so long.

"I've no interest in a mere sword."

And so the girl met one more deity.

"Here we go…Here we go."

After Demeter and Hephaistos were done treating Aiz as their toy, the girl and Loki exited Central Park and arrived at one corner of East Main Street.

Raising her face in exhaustion, Aiz saw a large tavern along the street.

It was built using brand-new materials from the doors up, so she could tell that it had recently been finished.

"Aiz, remember this place. Now and in the future, this shop'll always take care of ya. I guarantee it."

Aiz tilted her head, not really comprehending Loki, who seemed to be in a good mood for some reason.

As if responding to her doubt, Loki continued.

"It was just built, though. This shop is the one and only place where you can relax and enjoy delicious alcohol in the hustle and bustle around here." She flashed an "okay" sign. "I guarantee it."

Aiz had no clue what proof she had that made her so sure.

Since she had no interest in alcohol, Aiz peered up at the shop's sign instead.

It read: THE BENEVOLENT MISTRESS.

"Barkeep! Ya got company!"

She entered with Loki, but the place was dark and deserted.

One person, a female dwarf so big Aiz couldn't believe her eyes, was at the counter polishing a glass.

"I told ya we're only open at night. How many times do I have to tell ya before ya get it, nincompoop?"

"Nah, nah, I wasn't plannin' to start day drinkin'!"

Aiz could sense a certain aura around the surly dwarf.

That's an adventurer, someone with real strength. Incredible. She has a presence like Finn or Gareth. Or maybe even stronger than theirs.

Not backing down, Loki switched to a soft, honey-tongued plea.

"Can you let us use yer place tonight? I'm beggin' ya, Mama Mia~."

"Yer making me sick. The first time was way better."

"But yer the mama here now. And our familia'll be regular customers for ya! So it'll be fiiine. Throw us a little somethin', pleeeeeease."

"Sheesh, I've barely got any employees, and we're up to our eyes in stuff to do."

The dwarf just snorted in response to Loki's flirty act that made even Aiz uncomfortable.

Suddenly, Aiz noticed someone else's presence. A staff member wearing a uniform came through the door behind the counter that looked like it went to the kitchen. It was a catgirl older than Aiz. She had gloomy eyes and a doll-like expression that seemed vaguely familiar.

"Ahnya! Bring all the alcohol we have. We've got a couple of troublemakers!"

After addressing the waitress who just came in, the dwarf came back to the pair.

"So, a new member?"

"That's right! This is our Aizuu!"

"Hmph, the Doll Princess, huh?"

The owner stared down at her. Apparently, rumors of her had even made it to this tavern.

"You shouldn't be adventurin' when yer that small. I'll let ya eat lots of delicious stuff today. Prepare yourself!" she said with a laugh, totally overpowering Aiz.

Gradually understanding why they had come here, she glanced over at Loki.

The vermilion-haired goddess smiled serenely.

"Today's a feast for Finn and the others, Aizuu. A celebration of everyone's hard work!"

"All right, then, as thanks for all your hard work—cheers!"

""Cheers!""

The clink of mugs resounded as Loki toasted the group.

After the sun had finished setting that night, the banquet that the goddess had promised began at The Benevolent Mistress.

"For goodness' sake, holding a party as soon as we get back…Let us know beforehand, at least."

"It's fine, Riveria! I just wanted to show my thanks for everything you kids have done! This is all I can really do!"

"Ha-ha! You sure you didn't just want to drink some yourself, Loki?" Finn joked.

"Hmph, it woulda been better if ye'd picked a different place to have it, though."

After heading back for a bit with Aiz, Loki had met up with the group returning to the manor after they took care of the incident in the city. She had dragged them back out, saying, *"We're goin' to a bar!"* in order to start the feast she had arranged.

The goddess had talked about how her cute little followers needed a chance to decompress after fighting day and night, but Aiz suspected that Finn's comment was probably accurate, too. It was common knowledge that she liked to drink, and she often had the smell of booze on her breath at the manor.

Aiz was sipping some fresh-squeezed juice at the same table as Finn and the others.

"I heard that, ya prune-faced dwarf! I can just toss ya out on yer ass if ya want."

Bang! A huge roast pig slammed down on the table in front of them.

Aiz jumped in surprise as the dwarf owner responded contemptuously to Gareth's whining.

"Oi, see if ye can, ya crappy barkeep. All ye did was get a little tall; don't go gettin' cocky!"

"Quit it, Gareth. The others are watching."

"Hey, Mia. Sorry for imposing on you at the last minute like this. Thank you."

"Yer damn straight. I'm not gonna hold back on the bill, either."

"I know. You started this shop with the money you made from being an adventurer, after all. We'll drink and eat to our hearts' content."

Aiz was shocked to see Gareth itching for a fight, but Riveria was just watching from the side like this was normal, and Finn shot the breeze with the owner like they were old friends.

"…That dwarf…Do you know her?"

"You could say that. *We can't escape her* might be more accurate…"

"Mia, the owner, used to be an adventurer. She's currently half-retired from her familia, but until just a little while ago, we worked with her a lot."

"Hmph, she's just a loose cannon. She only knew how to brute-force her way through things."

"Heh-heh, lonely now that you don't have her to argue with all the time, Gareth?"

"Don't be stupid, Finn."

Sensing some connection between them, Aiz decided to ask, but she was even more surprised by the answer.

"She was an adventurer...but she opened a bar...?"

"Yes...When we first heard it, our jaws dropped."

Gareth smiled wryly as he started to down his entire mug and Finn's blue eyes narrowed.

"I think her intentions were wonderful, though."

"...?"

"The reason she opened this bar. She wanted a place where anyone could laugh and drink despite all the unrest in Orario. She stepped away from her familia in order to make that place possible."

"A place to laugh and eat, no matter how shitty the times." After hearing the owner's catchphrase and this bar's motto, Aiz looked around.

Other than the members of *Loki Familia*, there were lots of other demi-humans. And there were people who looked like average workers and a group of craftsmanlike blacksmiths in addition to the adventurers. Laughing aloud, drinking beer, savoring delicious food.

The gloomy atmosphere she'd noticed in the city during the day was nowhere to be found. Everyone looked like they were enjoying themselves without a care. It was a stereotypical lively bar scene.

...Warm.

Honestly, Aiz didn't really care much about the feast, but she did think that this was a comfortable place.

The scene before her eyes overlapped with one from her past.

Her father's concern as he got stuck with the bill while his friends drank and sang and danced. Aiz and her mom laughing as they watched. Memories of bygone days and a sense of nostalgia pierced deep into her chest...but Loki started making a big commotion, having a drinking competition with the lower-tier familia members, and the thoughts were swept away.

Because just like the sign said, this was The Benevolent Mistress.

"Aiz, don't just drink—have something to eat, too. Give me your plate."

"You've really gotten used to that, haven't you, Riveria?"

"Ga-ha-ha! She sure has."

"Don't tease me, you two."

Aiz was slowly picking away at her plate full of salad and steamed fish as the elites continued their conversation when all of a sudden, some of the other familia members burst over to the table.

"Aiiiiiiz! Why don't you hang out with us instead of the captain and those guys for once?"

"?!"

"Go for it, Kevin!"

The others didn't normally talk to Aiz, since she always seemed so cold, but thanks to the power of alcohol, they had apparently drummed up the courage to try tonight. Well and truly buzzed, they gathered around Aiz's seat for the party. The mysterious new member of the familia had been almost like a mascot, a sort of rare human, so they had been curious about her since long before.

Aiz was overwhelmed by the storm of attention.

"Aizuu, I mean Aiz! Want to try my delicious magic drink?" "Hey! You guys! What are you trying to get her to drink?!" "Relax, Riveria, every once in a while is fine." "If you drink this amazing little thing, you'll get stronger!"

"Stronger?"

She couldn't follow everything as all their conversations overlapped, but she perked up when she heard the words *you'll get stronger*. Naive, or perhaps a bit airheaded, she took the glass that was handed to her.

Finn winced and turned a blind eye while Gareth stroked his beard, seeming to enjoy himself as Aiz raised the fruity-smelling mystery drink (fruit wine) to her lips and drank it.

"........."

"How is it, Aiz?! Delicious, right?!"

"It feels good, right? So talk with us some!"

"...Huh? Aiiiz?"

"You okay...?"

As they got carried away, Aiz stopped responding. Holding the empty glass in both hands, she placed it on the table with a *thunk*.

"...Aiz?"

"Aizuu?"

Riveria and Loki both looked suspiciously at her, but the next moment—

Slash.

"Guaaaaaaaaaaaaaah?!"

"K-Kevin?!"

"She got Kevin!"

Holding her trusted sword, the tiny girl cut down one of the familia members crowding around her.

"Whoa, Aiz?!"

"...*Hic...*"

"Kyaaa?!"

"...*Hic...*"

"Noooooooooo?!"

"She's drunk?!"

"Someone grab her sword!"

"...*Hic...*"

"Waaaaaaaah?!"

"She got someone else?!"

Hiccupping cutely as she went, she unleashed a scathing slash.

The red-faced little girl cut down one adventurer from the city's largest familia after another.

The power of alcohol transformed her. Her golden eyes were drowsy and droopy, and there was no consciousness visible in them. There was only pure swordsmanship.

The lively bar descended into chaos because of the drunken young swordswoman. Blood literally flew amid the shrieking and yelling, and familia members collapsed one after the other. Chairs and tables were cut to pieces, and fragments soared through the air. Screams started to spread to the other customers when they noticed the extraordinary turn of events. It was like a vision of hell.

At the sight, time stopped for Finn, Gareth, Riveria, and Loki.

"Th-that's...Drunken Blade!"

"Ye've heard of this, Loki?!"

"I just made up the name, but it's definitely that! It's a forbidden technique where ya start slicin' things at random!"

"You can tell that just by looking?! Stop her, Gareth!"

Riveria lost her cool and shouted at Gareth and Loki's stupid jokes as she jumped up, sending her chair flying. Sweating nervously, Finn and Gareth stood and started to close in on the little girl who was swinging her sword all around.

"You stupid girl!"

But before they could move, the dwarf owner somehow appeared behind the girl and grabbed the raised sword with her bare hand.

With just two fingers.

"...Hic...?"

"Drink all ya want, but don't get carried away...That's the rule in here. Remember it."

Unable to move the sword at all, Aiz looked behind her in a drunken wonder. After the owner, Mia, gave the warning in her deathly cool voice, her eyes snapped open.

"Don't break store property—*you dumbasssssssssssssssssss*!!"

"Ugyuuuu?!"

An iron fist of anger cracked across the back of the little girl's head.

It was far stronger than the one Riveria had unleashed on her, and Aiz went down in one hit. The sword clattered lifelessly to the ground.

Loki's face turned white. Riveria's cheeks twitched. Finn and Gareth had adopted a thousand-yard stare. The shop fell quiet. The other staff and guests, everyone quivered as the furious ogress stood in the middle of the bar.

Just before she blacked out, Aiz was sobered up by the tremendous force of the blow, and right before she embraced the floor, she had one thought.

—I should never misbehave here.

That day, a new cardinal rule was passed down to the members of *Loki Familia*: Never let Aiz have alcohol.

Likewise, the unwritten rule that guests must never get carried away at The Benevolent Mistress spread among its customers.

CHAPTER 4

THOSE WHO REMAIN, THOSE LEFT BEHIND

Aiz froze in place.

She was at a loss for words, unmoving, even forgetting to breathe as she stood in front of it.

"This…is…"

Before her eyes was a jet-black scale, the size of a grown man's upper body, almost like a giant polished piece of obsidian.

Her heart raced.

It was the third day of their stay in the village.

A festival to pray for a plentiful harvest was beginning. With the rain lifting, people were hard at work preparing for the celebration. Aiz and Bell were also helping out, as thanks for taking care of them. It was her first time interacting with anyone outside of the village elder's home, and she was feeling out of place as the adults watched her and the children tried to get to know her. But they were all kind and smoothly broke the ice. Aiz smiled so many times as she helped out with the preparations.

This is a nice village.

Just as she was thinking that, it appeared before her eyes.

It was enshrined in a decorated little stone hut.

Its outline was elliptical, but with fragments missing.

Aiz's skin crawled under the aura emanating from its jet-black surface.

One villager noticed her shocked gaze as she stood stock-still on the road. Then, as if guessing what she was thinking, they spoke up.

"Miss Adventurer…That's a scale from Lord Black Dragon."

Aiz couldn't believe what she was hearing.

"Lord…Black Dragon?"

An ancient dragon also known as the one-eyed dragon.

The strongest of all the monsters that had emerged across the land in the Ancient Times. One of the targets of the Three Great Quests; something the world longed to see defeated. The two great familias led by Zeus and Hera had struck down Behemoth, the Terrestrial Tyrant, and Leviathan, the Ruler of the Sea, but the final one, the Black Dragon, defeated the world's strongest adventurers. Thrusting the world into the depths of despair, this creature was the source of darkness that gave rise to the Evils. Even now, that legendary dragon was still living somewhere at the edges of the Earth.

It was currently sleeping, but the day it would rise from slumber was said to be the beginning of the end times, the trigger of destruction.

Everyone on Earth wished for the defeat of the Black Dragon.

It was the duty demanded of Orario.

Even Aiz knew that.

There was no one who didn't.

However, for some reason, that embodiment of calamity was being worshipped in this village.

"It's said that long ago, when Lord Black Dragon was driven out of Orario, it crossed through the sky above this village, scattering countless scales as it passed."

"...!"

"Monsters don't approach because they are scared of those scales. They allow us to live in safety...Those scales are essentially our guardian deity."

The villager was talking about the vestigial aura of the ancient dragon emanating from the scales. The presence of the being that reigned supreme over all monsters. Monsters could naturally sense it and would not approach it out of fear. Thanks to that, this village was able to live in peace.

Aiz was shocked.

She had thought it was strange. They were in the depths of the Beor Mountain Range, where monsters roamed free, and yet there were no disturbances at all.

The scales were protecting Edas Village.

"Of course we know about the Three Great Quests...I assure you, we who are protected by Lord Black Dragon understand better than anyone that it must be defeated or the world will eventually be destroyed. Nonetheless, we can't not worship it, and we can't cease praying to it."

The villager lowered his eyes, clasped his hands together in a practiced ritual, and raised a prayer.

Being protected...by monsters...?

Not adventurers. Not gods.

An evil, hideous, cruel monster.

Moaning softly, she felt her entire world go askew.

Monsters were the enemy of all people. Absolute evil that brought only sadness and tears. That's what Aiz had believed. She had kept swinging her sword up until this day because she believed that.

And yet, an existence that must be destroyed was protecting her fellow people.

Her entire system of values was rocked. That one fundamental truth had been overturned, and her mind was overcome with nausea.

—A village where faith in the dragon had taken root.

A world that Aiz hadn't known.

It was a side of the truth that she would have been better off not knowing.

Beasts have to...be destroyed... The monsters, all the monsters... The dragon...

She couldn't control the wild surge of emotions.

A monster protecting people. She couldn't begin to process such an oxymoron.

A monster that coexists with people couldn't exist.

If Aiz acknowledged it, the determination she put into her raised sword—her entire raison d'être—would waver.

Because Aiz's sword could not be anything other than a tombstone for monsters.

The wave of sadness that had broken through the dam in her heart was vying with the flames of hatred in her chest.

Aiz saw a vision of Edas Village in flames overlaid with scenes of monsters destroying her home, taking their land, tearing up the earth. The dragon's scale before her eyes made her heart tremble and evoked the image of the root of all that suffering.

"M-Miss Adventurer...?"

"—!"

She was drawn back to reality by the villager's trembling voice. Without realizing it, she had grabbed the hilt of her Desperate and was clutching it so hard that it quivered, as if she might draw it at any moment.

She managed to peel her fingers out of their death grip on the hilt.

"...I'm sorry. I'm going...to walk a bit."

"O-okay..."

Excusing herself, she left the scale.

She walked through the center of the village, casting a sidelong glance at all the people smiling and continuing the preparations for the festival. There was more than one jet-black scale. Either several had fallen nearby or else the villagers had broken the one into pieces. She suspected the former, given their faith and the hardness of the scales. Most of the scales were around the outside of Edas Village, running along the edge of the forest like stone monuments.

Each time she found one, she would stare at it, motionless, her hands clenched.

Each time it took a Herculean feat of will to keep from drawing her sword.

Even if the black blaze threatened to consume her, she had to turn a blind eye to it for the sake of the people of the village. For the people smiling and laughing in the village next to the enshrined dragon's scale. For the impossible image of beasts living next to people without attacking. She didn't have to agree. That's what she kept telling herself.

Time passed and the sky turned red in the dusk.

The sun was about to sink below the western summit as night approached.

Aiz returned to the first scale she had found as the village was bathed in a warm sunset.

It was right near the center of the village.

Inside the decorated hut was an altar. Food was placed before the scale in offering. Before a piece of the dragon, worshipped and feared by the villagers.

Before a fragment of calamity that would destroy the world.

"Miss Aiz?"

Bell called out to her from behind.

She hadn't reacted to his approach, so he stopped behind her. She didn't have the composure to acknowledge him.

She continued to silently focus on the scale before her eyes without turning, so he couldn't see her face.

Finally, Bell spoke up and said the first thing that came to his mind.

"It's almost like a god, don't you think?"

In that moment—

The black inferno in Aiz's heart flared. Gripped by an intense emotion that blurred her vision, she spat out a denial.

"That thing is no god."

The heavy, cold, and sharp tone of voice she used surprised even her.

Swordlike, as if it would cut through everything.

"_____"

She could tell that the boy behind her was at a loss for words. He was taken aback by the intense emotion she had displayed, the glimpse of darkness she had laid bare.

"..."

Sensing the boy's fear, Aiz lowered her eyes slightly.

She couldn't allow herself to direct her black rage at the innocent boy. She managed to reclaim at least that much of her senses. The fire within was tamped down, and her emotions came under control.

When she turned back around, she was wearing the aloof mask of the Sword Princess again.

"Let's go back."

"...S-sure."

Aiz turned around and walked away from the hut.

Frozen in place by the exchange, Bell rushed to follow after her.

Walking beside her, he peeked at her face from the side but didn't try to ask her anything. His expression looked like he had crossed the border from reality to illusion and didn't know what to think anymore.

That's fine, Aiz thought. *Please don't ask me anything. If you press me, I'm not sure that I can control myself, and I don't know what might come out.*

The distance between them was immeasurable.

It could never, ever be bridged.

Aiz felt like the boy's existence had moved impossibly far away from hers in an instant.

Or rather, she had cut herself off from the rest of the world.

In the village sunset, enclosed in its own little world, Aiz felt that she was alone.

Regaining control over her emotions was difficult.

Separating herself from everyone, closing her eyes, and touching Desperate while soothing the blaze in her heart, she finally obtained some peace of mind.

She withdrew from the ongoing preparations for the festival, returned to the village elder's home, and stood by the window, staring outside. There were several large logs tied together in the plaza. They were clearly going to be lit and used for a bonfire.

She silently looked out on the village protected by the dragon and the constant cheer leading up to the festival.

"Do you hate this village?"

"!"

The person who spoke was the village elder, Kam.

Aiz was shocked. The elderly man had come without his daughter, Rina. Standing beside her, he joined her in looking out the window.

"It seems your eyes have changed since this morning."

"Th-that's…"

No, she could have said, *of course not*. She tried to deny it, but the words wouldn't come.

Ignoring Aiz's stammered attempts to respond, Kam continued without seeming to mind.

"This village is protected by the dragon's scale. It's surely heretical to anyone observing it from the outside."

"I…"

"It wouldn't be strange for you to judge us. As an adventurer who slays monsters…and as someone who must have lost something important to them."

"!"

Aiz's eyes opened wide.

Kam smiled, looking out the window, his words slow and careful, as if he knew what she was thinking.

"At first, I also…hated this village."

"Eh…?"

The elderly human answered Aiz's confusion.

"It's a bit embarrassing, but I was originally a member of a certain goddess's familia…Unfortunately, I couldn't protect her and lost her. Falling into despair, I entered the Beor Mountains intending to die."

Aiz could tell by looking at his face, lit by the setting sun, and the fond reminiscence in his eyes that he had loved that goddess.

"However, I arrived in this village. At first, I was furious with the people here who saved me. Why wouldn't they just let me die?"

"Is that…why you…hated it…?"

"Yes, but…the people here wouldn't give up on me. I tried to shut myself off from everything, but they took my hand…

"…And I was saved. Despite giving up on the world, I still let my tears flow."

Kam described his experience to her with a tranquil smile.

"All the people of this village are scarred, other than the ones born here. We were driven out of the worlds we lived in before, drowning in despair; our tears dried up…"

"…"

"Maybe we're all just licking our wounds. But I think it's thanks to them…"

Looking out at the village, the old man's eyes narrowed.

"…that I wasn't *alone*."

Ah, that's—

As the door of memories opened in Aiz's heart, Kam looked at her.

"Aiz…You remind me of myself."

"…"

"I'm sorry if my saying all this bothers you. Just consider it the ramblings of an old man."

That's when Aiz realized that even with the sunset's light covering it, Kam's face looked much paler than when they had first met.

She gasped, but Kam continued without breaking his smile.

"I pray someone will eventually fill the hole in your heart that hasn't yet healed."

Aiz was silent for a while.

Before the old man in the twilight, she could offer no denials or pretenses. All she could do was look back at him.

Kam had said he wasn't alone.

However, he was still pained by his loss even now.

His prayer seemed almost like a plea for her to not end up like him.

Keeping silent, unsure what she should say, she eventually voiced the only words that came to mind.

"…Thank you…very much."

That night after the sun set.

Edas Village's festival began just as planned.

Centered around a large bonfire, the villagers were milling cheerfully with drinks in one hand and food in the other. The children seemed to be excited by the festive atmosphere, running around among the adults who were sipping their alcohol. With all the various races of demi-humans in the village, the unusually high percentage of halfs was noticeable.

"Um, are you okay, Goddess? You really shouldn't force yourself…"

"I'm fine! Since you two took such good care of me, there's no reason not to be fine!"

Hestia smiled in response to Bell's concerned look.

Perhaps because she was feeling better after three days' rest, she decided to tag along to the festival that Aiz and Bell had been helping out with. She was wearing some clothes of Rina's from when she was younger, an outfit that matched Aiz's except for the blue to contrast with her red.

Rina had even teased them about how they looked like sisters when they stood next to each other.

...Hestia's gotten better...Maybe tomorrow we can...

Aiz was thinking about next steps as *Hestia Familia*'s cheerful conversation went on beside her.

Before, she'd had mixed feelings about this village, so she'd wanted to leave before she got any more confused. She'd be lying if she denied that. But now, she wasn't quite so sure.

Her mind was less agitated and more simply unstable.

Her legs felt a little wobbly, like she wasn't standing on solid ground.

She had calmed down significantly after talking to Kam, but she still felt disconnected from the events around her.

She watched the bonfire's flames rise into the darkness with Bell and Hestia.

The word *gorgeous* slipped from her lips to describe the totally natural light, unlike the magic-stone lanterns she knew.

"Ah, Lady Hestia!"

"Are you feeling better already?!"

The villagers gathered around them.

People were worried after hearing about her from Kam. Among them were several who had come by the residence to share medicinal herbs to help with her recovery.

There weren't any deities in Edas Village, so young and old, men and women alike all gathered around Hestia. Young children in particular were filled with curiosity and wonder. Hestia was overwhelmed at first, but she eventually cracked a smile and started thanking them.

Then.

"Hmm...?"

They could hear a song.

The villagers' merry voices and claps created music, and couples had gathered around the bonfire at some point and started to dance.

"Is that the village's traditional dance? Most of the children there seem young, though..."

"Ah, you see...I wouldn't say it's the village's law or anything, but when an unmarried man asks a woman for a dance at this festival, it's sort of like a confession. It's said that if she accepts, they will be blessed with a lifetime of happiness..."

"O-oh?"

"Goddess! Since this is a festival for fertility, we'd love to have you dance with us, if you feel up to it!"

"Please bless us with a boon!"

Hestia had started to fidget nervously at the response to her question. When they started asking her for a blessing, she cleared her throat.

"Ahem. Um, Bell? It's a bit sudden, but I have to take care of my godly duties here, it seems...So, um, yeah."

Lit by the warm glow of the bonfire, the goddess looked restless as she glanced flirtatiously at him.

"If you'll dance with me...maybe we can call *that incident* water under the bridge?"

Aiz could tell she meant the fight Bell had mentioned the other day. The villagers around them cheered her on as Bell blinked repeatedly before flushing—trying to keep from going slack-jawed—and nodding.

For some reason, Aiz couldn't look away from the exchange.

"All right...Let's dance, Goddess."

"Do it right, Bell. Like you did with Wallensomething...I heard you danced with her at Apollo's banquet."

Aiz seemed puzzled when she was suddenly a part of the conversation for some reason.

She tilted her head in confusion, but she understood what the goddess was trying to say.

"You probably gave some flowery, pretentious invitation, right? I want to really dance with you, too."

She must have been talking about the time Aiz and Bell had danced at a certain banquet. Apparently, Hestia hadn't gotten a chance to dance with Bell back then, so it would be fair to say that it was her turn this time.

The villagers cheered while Bell turned red and fidgeted.

Aiz watched their exchange without blinking.

Bell was sweating bullets, caught between Hestia and Aiz...But seeming to make up his mind, he held his hand out to the goddess.

"...C-could I please...have this dance, Goddess?"

"Yes!"

Taking the boy's hand as he blushed, she led him toward the resplendent bonfire.

The villagers cheered. The sparks danced through the air as if welcoming them.

They held hands and improvised a folk dance, and Hestia laughed pleasantly as Bell responded with a strained laugh. He seemed somehow happy, though.

"..."

The pair danced happily together.

Just a little bit, Aiz felt a sting in her heart.

Aiz told herself that it was because she'd seen that dragon scale.

That black flame hidden in her heart had flared up again, reminding her of her past deeds.

But all of a sudden, she realized it wasn't that.

Ah...That's wrong.

I'm lonely...

Aiz all of a sudden understood the true nature of the empty feeling in her heart.

Lefiya, Tiona, Tione...Riveria, none of them is here. I'm by myself.

And on top of that, there was the beast's scale she just couldn't understand, which made everything worse. Knowing the origin of the village and hearing Kam's story, she still felt uneasy, as if she might lose sight of herself.

Her current feelings were an extension of all that. Ill at ease, Aiz was the only one who couldn't join in with the bustle and celebration of the festival. She alone was different, even now wearing her aloof Sword Princess mask.

At that point in time, Aiz was truly *alone*.

It reminded her of the sense of solitude she had often felt during that first year after meeting Riveria, Gareth, and Finn. The one anchor she had here, Bell and Hestia, was gone, too...She was at a loss.

I...don't belong here.

Still watching their dance, Aiz secretly moved away.

No...I shouldn't be here.

Distancing herself from the ring of villagers, she approached a house, becoming a wallflower as she tried to hide.

People's laughter. The bright dancing of the flames. A human girl holding hands with her father, an animal-person boy who was getting a scolding from his mother for being too rowdy. It was a heartwarming scene, almost like a scene from a book brought to life for Aiz. The house's shadow fell over her like a cold embrace.

No one called out to her. As if deciding she would just be a hindrance to everyone else's enjoyment, she made herself unnoticeable.

Not being found by anyone had long been a specialty for her.

She hadn't even been found by her hero, after all.

Such a self-deprecating observation was unusual for Aiz. And just as she made it...

"—Um, Miss Aiz."

Her heart fluttered in shock as someone called her name. She struggled to maintain her mask before the boy who had found her after his dance with Hestia had ended.

Acting as if everything was normal, she paused a second before responding.

"...Yes?" She stared out at the plaza after glancing at him. "Everyone looks like they're having fun..."

The jealous words unexpectedly slipped from her mouth, as if the smiles among the villagers' faces had stirred them up inside her.

It's Bell's fault.

It's his fault I realized it.

She was jealous.

She had even managed to lie to herself.

Her eyes narrowed as she watched the storybook come to life, as if it was blindingly bright. Taking care not to look at him, she responded with a bit of a pout.

"…Your dance was very good."

"Eh?…Th-thank you."

"…You're…a great dancer."

"Ah, thanks…"

"…"

"…"

The conversation broke off.

Why had she run her mouth about that? Aiz didn't really understand it herself.

She could only conclude that something really was weird about her at the moment.

"Ah…um, are you not going to dance?"

"Everyone…seems like they are having fun…I don't want to ruin their moment…"

"You won't!"

"And…I have no one to dance with."

—Like a child.

The other Aiz buried in her heart softly whispered.

That's exactly right.

Aiz thought as she looked down.

"If…if I'm good enough for you…"

Her eyes widened upon hearing his nervous voice, and she finally looked at Bell.

His cheeks were bright red.

"…You'll dance…with me?"

With someone like me?

With a doll-like person like me who doesn't belong in a world like this?

Those questions lingering in her eyes as she looked at him, the boy got even redder and started behaving even more strangely.

"Uh, yes, that is, if you are okay with it…?"

Gazing back at his rubellite eyes, Aiz nervously reached out to take his hand—.

"—*Boom!*"

"Ah."

"Urghhh!"

Rushing in from the side, the goddess's tackle nailed Bell right in the ribs.

"What's this, Wallensomething? You have no one to dance with?! Then allow me to dance with you!"

"…Thank you?"

She blinked in surprise as Hestia grabbed her hand and dragged her away.

Leaving Bell writhing on the ground, she led Aiz next to the base of the warm, bright bonfire.

"Sheesh, you really are cunning! Don't think I'll let you tempt my Bell!"

"I—I'm sorry…?"

All she could do was apologize in response to Hestia's glare.

Joining hands, they stepped into the dance ring.

"So are you worrying about something?"

"Eh…"

"You've been lost in thought ever since that time you came to make Bell take a break, haven't you? I'm a goddess, after all. Of course I'd notice."

It was Aiz's biggest surprise that day.

Hestia sounded a little sullen as she tried to begin the dance.

"It would be a pain if I overstepped and then got Loki on my case…"

"…"

"But you look like you're lost right now. And unfortunately, I can't just ignore children like that. D-don't misunderstand! It's not because I want to help you!"

Pulled along by Hestia's lead, Aiz was almost dragged off her feet, but she barely managed to keep her balance. Raising her face, she saw that the goddess was watching her, waiting.

"...I.." She timidly began to speak. "I just...felt like I was truly alone..."

"..."

"Learning about this village...I got scared..."

She knew she wasn't putting it into words well and was almost incoherent. But as she looked into those blue eyes, her mouth kept moving. "Are you...not scared? Of someone leaving you behind...?"

"Leaving me behind?"

"...Something important...disappearing before your eyes...?"

It was the first time she had asked a deity something like that. But she had always wanted to know. Kam's face flashed through her mind—the face of an old man who felt the pain of losing something important like she had.

Yes.

Gods who lived *forever* would always know the *separation* that accompanied any of their relationships.

Hestia was someone who would lose people. Someone who would be left behind.

Aiz knew loss already. She had already been left behind.

That emptiness in her heart resembled the solitude of eternity.

She was asking if an eternity of pain and sadness wasn't scary.

"...If I said it wasn't scary, I'd be lying. Or maybe *lonely* is a better way to put it? Interacting with you children down here...Our love lasts but a moment."

Hestia continued her slow, rocking dance as she responded. Aiz's eyes opened wide at her response.

"But we're actually pretty shameless, and we try to make our bonds with children last forever."

"Eh?"

Her cheeks reddening, Hestia smiled with all her heart. Like a mischievous child.

"Anyway, you guys can make a bond that lasts forever with anyone, you know?"

Aiz was taken aback as the goddess continued as if revealing a secret magic spell.

"Think back to all the memories you have, starting from when you met. If the memory of a special someone makes you smile, then that's your eternal bond."

"That's…"

Hestia's magic was a little too simple, so the girl felt somewhat disappointed as her hopes were dashed.

And with that disappointment came pain and sadness.

"Wallensomething, I think that memories are living things."

"…?"

"Memories that you can't forget contain joy. They continue on in you forever, and you can always hold them close. There are important things left behind for you there."

"!"

"When you get sad, you can cling to them as you break down in tears. They can encourage you, make you smile…And when you're lost, they can help you remember what's important."

The sparks danced through the air as if wrapping Hestia and Aiz in a holy light.

"And forgotten memories are happy things, too. Instead of always being sad and relying on them, you can face forward and laugh with the people around you."

Aiz was drawn in to the goddess's smile.

This was all from the point of view of a goddess, of course. People on Earth could certainly hurt themselves by clinging to memories, too.

But she wasn't entirely wrong, either.

Even in Aiz's memories—

"You feeling a bit better now?"

"…Yes."

"Then let's dance! It'd be a waste not to enjoy yourself just because you think you're alone!"

As Aiz nodded, Hestia responded with an innocent laugh.

The two began dancing.

Long black and golden hair swirled through the air, sparkling in the light of the bonfire. The dance between the beautiful goddess and the beautiful girl received the most cheers of any that night.

Everyone smiled as they watched the two, including Rina and Bell. Lots of people called out, and to Aiz's surprise, her solitude disappeared.

Surrounded by laughter, Aiz felt her lips—ever so slightly—curl into a smile.

After the village's festival ended.

Aiz, Hestia, and Bell gathered at the edge of the village.

"Ugh, I got a little carried away…I feel kinda shaky."

"Th-that's why I told you to take it easy!"

The village kids had begged her to keep dancing, so Hestia had obliged for the whole night.

Aiz smiled ever so slightly as Bell chided the goddess.

In the plaza, the villagers were sleeping off their drunken stupor.

"Anyway, about what to do next…"

"Yeah, I'm good to go. I'm sorry for causing so much trouble, but I can walk just fine now."

As Bell started to talk about next steps, Hestia entrusted that judgment to the top-tier adventurer. Aiz nodded.

"Tomorrow morning…we'll leave the village."

Saying that, Aiz was surprised to notice that she was a little bit reluctant to leave.

She had no idea what had caused that change of heart, but Aiz had started to think that maybe it wasn't such a bad thing to dwell on memories a little bit.

Almost nine years after she had taken up her sword in Orario, she felt like she could begin facing all the feelings she had forgotten in the turbulent days of fighting—the impatience, the sadness, the tears, the smiles.

Her lips started to break into a new smile of their own.

"—Lady Hestia!"

That was when Rina interrupted, rushing toward them.

Aiz had a bad feeling as the girl looked like she was about to break down in tears. As if confirming her suspicions, a monster's howl echoed from the forest's depths.

Rina's voice quivered as she held her chest, holding back tears.

"Would you…see my father off…on his journey to heaven?"

"…Eh?"

Aiz wasn't sure whether the soft cry of surprise came from Bell, or Hestia, or even herself.

But all she could think was—*Nothing lasts forever.*

A feeling of emptiness gnawed at her heart.

THE WIND'S DESIRED ETERNITY

Гэта казка іншага сям і

Назаўжды абматаць жаданне

Everything was going smoothly. Aiz gained much under Finn's leadership, from Riveria's teachings, and through Gareth's admonishments.

Having run out of tears to shed, Aiz threw herself into battle day in and day out. And day by day, she started forgetting how to smile, but even so, she showed growth in many areas as they watched over her.

The city was as turbulent as always, and she could hear the siren's song of destruction and chaos, but she still kept running without losing sight of herself.

She felt fulfilled in those days.

Everything was going smoothly—or at least it should have been.

Aiz Wallenstein

LEVEL 1

Strength: D591 -> D593 Endurance: D559
Dexterity: B788 Agility: A800 -> 801 Magic: I0

Aiz furrowed her brows.

Looking at the update sheet Loki handed her, she unconsciously clenched her fist.

"Aiz, this is the same path everyone has followed. Don't take it too hard."

"As you master your ability, your rate of development naturally decreases. It's not like you have no more room to grow."

"Yeah. That's just how Statuses work."

Finn, Riveria, and Loki were all offering encouragement, but it went in one ear and out the other.

Aiz's Status had plateaued. After her strength had seemed to go up by leaps and bounds every day, it had suddenly stopped.

Now, day after day after day, her growth had been limited to these small boosts that might as well have been rounding errors. It was almost as if she had reached her limit.

Aiz was getting impatient.

Up until now, she had felt herself actually getting stronger and improving. Even the strategy and techniques that Finn had drilled into her had proven their value. All of it had been reflected in the numbers going up on her Status. Those numbers proved she was on the right path, and the more they went up, the more confident she could feel in her progress.

However, now—

It's too low...

The upper bound for her base abilities—in other words, her proficiency in a given field—was 999.

That was the upper bound for Aiz based on her race.

The winter one year after she entered *Loki Familia*, Aiz hit a wall.

"...Level up."

When those two words crossed her lips, the others' faces tensed.

"What do I need...to level up...?"

Level up. The spiritual container's sublimation. The one process that existed for surpassing the limits that had been placed on her body and moving to a higher realm.

Riveria responded to the girl's question.

"...Leveling up is not something that an adventurer simply just does. There are steps you have to go through."

"Ye just need to keep goin' through the labyrinth like you have been. I know it's frustrating, but that's the fastest way."

"You can't get impatient here, Aiz. You have to go deliberately and carefully."

Gareth, Riveria, and Finn all expressed the same opinion.

"There is no point in rushing it. We have all seen countless adventurers get impatient like you are now and then self-destruct when they could not control that impatience. So just calm yourself, Aiz."

What are you saying? This isn't a joke.

Aiz couldn't help feeling that their statements were an attempt to hold her back.

I want to get strong. I need to get strong. I don't have time to be standing still.

It was the first wall she had encountered, and even if she couldn't see it, she could feel it blocking her path. And their responses just fanned the flames of her impatience. It was an expression of her fear that she might have reached the limits of her growth.

The unease she felt welling up turned into anger as she looked away. Clenching the update paper in her fist, she stormed out of the office.

"...Riveria, about tellin' Aizuu how to level up..."

"I won't tell her. There's no way I could."

After Aiz had left...

Riveria looked down as she responded to Loki's question.

"Yeah, I guess so," the goddess mumbled, resting her hands behind her head.

"Leveling up requires high-level excelia. That means a great accomplishment...something you can only achieve by adventuring."

"Defeating an opponent far stronger than you, delving deeper into the Dungeon and facing death countless times...Those are the last things we should be letting Aiz do. Like Riveria said, she would charge in, do something reckless, and get herself hurt or worse."

Finn and Gareth picked up after Riveria left off. Their anguish was audible.

It was hiding in the shadows now, but Aiz's tendency to not care about herself had not been eliminated. She was still perfectly content to risk life and limb in order to prioritize her wish.

On an adventure where her life was at risk, it was a land mine waiting to be stumbled onto.

"But still, we can't let things stay this way, ya know? Aizuu's just buildin' up more stress and might just blow as it is. So what are ya gonna do about it?"

Loki wouldn't let them escape from the reality of the situation or delay the inevitable. Of the three followers entrusted with the growth of their familia's newer members and pioneering deeper into the Dungeon, Riveria responded first with a firm rejection.

"We should not treat her any differently from the others. She can target monsters of a similar or higher level as a member of a party. Even if that takes more time and effort."

Gareth and Finn nodded in agreement.

"There's little we can do when it comes to the 'great accomplishment' she would need."

"All we can do is make sure she adventures safely, though I admit that's an odd turn of phrase."

Loki reluctantly accepted their unanimous judgment.

She narrowed her eyes slightly, looking past the door Aiz had just stormed out, then shifted topics to change the mood.

"Finn, when was the deadline for the expedition mission again?"

"Mm, with an extension, maybe in one month? Royman was bugging me about it yesterday."

"Speakin' of unreasonable requests, take a look at what the Guild is askin'. We have to face down those Evils bastards, protect the peace, aye, and don't forget the expedition to unexplored territory, not to mention everything else."

Gareth sighed and grumbled about their workload.

It was *Loki Familia*'s job as the strongest faction and thus the representative of Orario. They didn't really have the time to be obsessing over the fate of one girl.

"They want a successor to Zeus and Hera as soon as possible. Someone with the influence and power to end this period of chaos… to be a symbol to calm the masses inside and outside the city. And that's our job, since we were the ones who ran them out of the city in the first place."

Finn's blue eyes narrowed as he clasped his hands on the desk.

He was also chasing his ambition. Torn between his duty as leader of the faction and his personal desire, he had to make concessions as he searched for the best response. He had the same wish as Aiz, but he displayed an adult's maturity that she lacked.

"What do you intend to do about Aiz? Will you bring her along, Finn?"

Riveria was also trying to balance her job as second-in-command and her role as teacher as best she could.

"…I'll wait and see. There's the obvious question of whether she's strong enough to contribute, but even before that, if she stays like this, I'm going to leave her aboveground."

Finn closed his eyes and shook his head.

"If we took her deeper into the Dungeon in this state, we might as well just perform her last rites now."

Golden eyes watched her father's back as he swung his sword.

She was sitting with her mother in the shade of a tree as the sun's warm rays filtered through.

He seemed embarrassed by people watching him practice, so he didn't like to do it in front of others. But when Aiz's mother coaxed him to let her watch, he would always give in. After his initial embarrassment, he would soon become engrossed in swinging his sword, and her mom would watch his gallant face with a smile. And Aiz's cheeks would always flush as the sight captivated her.

She couldn't keep up with the blurred blade. But she could still tell how beautiful his techniques were. His lower body hardly moved as he swung the sword freely in all directions, as if it were a conductor's baton. Sometimes he would take a big step in and spin around, making a silver arc through the air. She could remember that sword's melody whenever she wanted by simply closing her eyes.

She loved seeing his techniques.

She knew that her father's sword was used for hurting things. And the flash of an unhesitating sword calling forth a mist of blood was a scary thought to her. But that was a sword for saving everyone.

A sword to protect her mother.

When she thought of that, she was proud of her father. She aspired to be like him.

He was the hero she dreamed of. The swordsman her mother loved.

Finally, after finishing his training, he came back to the shade of the tree.

She beamed at him as he approached, and he returned her smile, the wind blowing his hair.

"Aiz."

He said her name and held out his sheathed blade to her.

After a moment of wide-eyed hesitation, she took the sword in both her hands.

It had a profound weight, but for some reason, it also felt comfortable to her.

Her father smiled as he watched her.

"Aiz."

Turning to face the voice coming from behind her, she saw her mother smiling as well.

Almost as if telling her to follow her father, she raised her arm, held up her finger, and made a sound.

"_____"

Along with the sound, Aiz felt a tender breeze embracing her body. She trembled, giggling as the wind's whispers tickled her.

Her mother broke into a smile and wrapped her arms around her and the wind.

"I'll always be with you."

This person. And me.

She nodded at the woman's words. She nodded over and over as she smiled…

As she basked in the warmth of her father and mother, happiness filled her.

The sword was calling her closer, and the wind was smiling so gently.

—And that was where her memories of the past cut out.

© Kiyotaka Haimura

✳   ✳   ✳

"…"

Feeling tears flowing down her cheeks, she opened her eyes. Aiz got up without speaking, rubbing her eyes as she sat atop the bed. All alone in the room as the remnants of the dream's warmth dissipated, she returned to cold reality.

Why now?

Why did I see that dream?

Aiz cursed herself, her memories, and the scenes of her past.

Why now, when she couldn't just forget everything by frantically rushing forward? When she was blocked by the wall that was her limit?

"…"

Outside the window was a gray morning sky in stark contrast to the scene from her dream. It was as if the world was expressing the feelings in her heart. After staring at that darkness for a moment, Aiz got out of bed and quickly changed. Reflected in the mirror in the corner of her room was the profile of a girl whose smile had died. The look of a doll who had smothered her feelings.

—It would have been better if it were all a dream.

That was what the girl in her heart whispered. The weak Aiz cowering in the darkness hugging her knees.

"…I have to fight."

Because those days were long past, and they would never come back.

That dream was followed by several days filled with unease and impatience.

She would descend into the Dungeon and slaughter more monsters with a more ghastly vigor than before, but she could not get past that wall. Her Status continued to stagnate. Riveria and the others accompanying her would scold her when she kept fighting without any pause for rest, and she heard them tenderly tell her to "calm down" countless times. From that point on, they had Aiz team up with other low-level followers in order to search the Dungeon as a party, but that just tortured Aiz even more as she started to suspect that it was a way to keep her from acting rashly.

Aiz heard the crackle of fire—the black flame flickering in her heart.

You have to get stronger. If you don't—

She broke out in an unpleasant sweat. Her heart trembled. Standing before the wall blocking her way, she felt more and more lost as her goal vanished before her eyes. As soon as she stopped moving, an icy loneliness would grip her.

The feeling of cowering alone in the darkness. Of being left behind by important people, of facing cold reality, of being abandoned by the world. The loneliness tearing her apart, accompanied by a flood of tears. She had papered over this abject emptiness with the will to fight for her wish, and now it was threatening to engulf that tiny body. The things that Riveria and the others were trying to help Aiz forget were starting to latch on to her.

She had to do something. She had to break open a path for herself.

Because Aiz knew that no help would come for her.

She realized that a hero wouldn't appear.

She would even let that disgusting black flame consume her if that was what it would take. She would never again be that child crying away all her feelings.

Aiz struggled. In order to avoid being ensnared by the weak little girl she had left behind.

Her trusted sword did not tell her anything as it continued to bathe in the blood of monsters.

It had been a while since she had visited a place this packed with adventurers.

Gareth and the others took care of selling her drop items. They used the establishments at Babel to take care of everything, including exchanging them for money.

Guild Headquarters was crowded with people returning from the Dungeon. While rounding up even more familias to send out to maintain the peace and stand against the rise of evil, they were also encouraging the Dungeon crawling necessary to obtain more magic stones to support Orario's industry. She was careful not to let her adult coworkers knock her over as she made her way through the lobby.

Aiz had come here by herself behind Riveria's back, searching for the secret to leveling up.

She had realized that they were hiding something about reaching the next phase of her spiritual container, because they wouldn't tell her anything about the actual method of leveling up and showed no intention of ever telling her. And they had sworn the other members of *Loki Familia* to the same secrecy.

She could try asking total strangers and other adventurers, but she knew that her fellow rookies were jealous of her. They either wouldn't give her a clue because she was ahead of them, or they'd lie to her. The malice hidden in the latter was her main concern. No matter how impatient she was, she was not yet desperate enough to risk something so stupid and careless. Raised as an adventurer by the likes of Riveria, Finn, and Gareth, she could not go that far.

Consequently, since Aiz had no connections with anyone outside the familia, the only place she had to turn to was here.

"Ummm..."

"Hi, how can I help y...? Wait, aren't you...Aiz Wallenstein?"

The red-haired receptionist at the window, the werewolf Rose Faunette, was visibly surprised by her unexpected guest. She had thought it was a prum adventurer at first, but just like the day they first met, she dropped her formal receptionist tone.

"It's been a while, hasn't it? You've sure become something. If I could have been your adviser, I'd probably have gotten a raise by now...Tch, I missed my chance."

"..."

"I thought the monsters would get you before long, but...I guess Riveria and those guys did a good job protecting you. Must be nice to be so loved."

It was just her nature, but Rose bluntly spoke her mind.

Businesslike—as if she was trying to maintain a distance between her and the adventurers she dealt with. Perhaps that was the secret to her success as a receptionist.

Watching Aiz silently acknowledge her small talk with an unchanging, aloof expression, the red-haired beauty shrugged.

"Okay, okay, I got it. So what do you need?"

Aiz finally spoke.

"Leveling up…How do I do it?"

Rose's brow furrowed in surprise, and her eyes met Aiz'z golden ones. She could see the black sparks of a girl willing to do whatever it would take to escape the corner she was trapped in.

"…Isn't it something that eventually comes from going down into the Dungeon?"

"Liar! Just tell me!"

"I'm not lying. It's the truth. That's what all the other adventurers do."

Rose maintained her flippant tone as Aiz leaned in, glaring at her. Her expression soon changed, though, and she looked down at the girl with a serious gaze.

"And even if I did know more…I wouldn't tell you as you are now."

"!"

"I don't want your blood on my hands."

The girl's doll-like mask slipped in her desperation when Rose hit her with that.

Aiz was gnawing at her lips, when—

"Ahhh, I've finally come back after my long journey! Were you lonely without me, Sofi?!"

"…?"

She heard an extremely loud laugh from another window.

Looking over, she saw a man—a god—with orange hair talking to a receptionist.

"I didn't notice you were gone. I'd have been fine if you never came back, honestly."

"Ahhh, yeah, I love it when a lovely elf gives me the cold shoulder! How's about we go on a date now?!"

"I've got work to do here, and you're getting in the way, so if you could just go back to wherever you came from and never return, I'd appreciate it."

The cold-looking silver-haired elf receptionist was particularly rough in rejecting the playboy god. She seemed rather experienced at doing it.

"Ah, that god's always like that. Though I guess you could say the same for all the gods who play around. Anyway, if you don't need anything else, head back to your familia. Lately the Evils have been acting suspiciously, so you shouldn't be loitering around by yourself."

As Aiz glanced over at the boisterous back-and-forth, Rose urged her to leave. Pursing her lips as the werewolf started taking care of another adventurer, she left Guild Headquarters.

Lately, it was as if the overcast skies were reflecting her clouded mind. Beneath that ashen sky, Aiz felt a whole new level of concern as her final hope failed.

She cut through the main branch's wide front garden when—

"Are you the Doll Princess?"

A familiar voice called out from behind her.

Turning around, the ridiculous god from before was walking toward her.

"I'm not totally up-to-date on things happening in Orario after being gone so long. To think a rookie like you would have shown up."

His eyes, the same color as his hair, were unmistakably focused on Aiz. Fingering the brim of his travel hat, the dandy god smiled.

Assuming it was just the meddling of a god looking to amuse himself, Aiz turned to ignore him as he chased after her, but...

"Weren't you asking about leveling up earlier?"

At those words, she stopped and faced him again.

"By chance, are you worried about growth after your Status hit its limit?"

"!"

"And no one will tell you how to level up, despite all your worries? That ring a bell?"

Aiz could only stare in shock as he kept putting all her thoughts into words.

His smile never changed as he finally stood eye to eye with her. He moved his face closer to hers, peering into her eyes.

"Looks like I'm onto something…Are you the one Zeus—?"

Thanks to her shock, she missed the second part that he murmured to himself.

He stood back up.

"Shall I tell you how to level up?"

"?!"

"I'd rather you not be so suspicious. Guiding children is a god's duty. That's just common sense, isn't it?"

"…Will you really…tell me?"

"I swear upon the things over which I preside: I won't lie."

Aiz didn't care anymore why the god had approached her or what he was trying to achieve.

She leaned in aggressively.

"Please tell me!"

"Sounds good. The hero who will bear the Era of Promise…It's best to raise the odds as much as possible, even if it's only a bit."

The god's smile deepened as he said the last part to himself.

"As for my name…Well, maybe not. It would probably be a pain if Loki found out. So I'd appreciate it if you didn't tell anyone about me." The dandy god added that clause to their deal.

Aiz impatiently accepted without a second thought.

In the middle of the relatively deserted front garden, the god whispered to her.

"The condition for sublimating our Blessing…is accomplishing great feats."

"Where are you, Aiz?!"

She could hear a voice calling her.

Aiz knew immediately it was Riveria.

It had been almost a full year since they had first met. She was always strict, sometimes kind, and very rarely warm. That clear, bell-like voice had reached her ears like a gentle touch countless times. It was almost always with her. That was why Aiz could guess what sort of face Riveria was making right now. However, despite knowing it, she pretended not to hear her.

Night enshrouded Orario, and the sound of falling rain engulfed the city.

Shivering in the cold winter downpour, Aiz walked toward the area lit by the magic-stone streetlight.

"Riveria..."

"Aiz...?!"

The sight that greeted her as she turned the corner left Riveria speechless.

Armor stained red, her battle dress in tatters. The rain washed away the blood, but it couldn't hide the deep red gashes in her skin. The girl who appeared beneath the magic-stone light was the image of a broken-down doll.

Aiz had not even remembered to put her trusted sword back into its scabbard. Her palms were bleeding after swinging it so much. She looked up at the shocked elf, but her face was blank, showing no emotion at all.

"I'd like a potion..."

Riveria had been searching for Aiz nonstop since she left the manor by herself. The elf's gorgeous jade hair that she had grown out was clinging to her face in the rain. She was at a loss for words.

"I'm going to the Dungeon *again*..."

When Aiz confessed what she had been doing, Riveria's face twisted.

"What are you doing?! What are you saying?!" she screamed, dashing toward Aiz and kneeling down in front of her.

She didn't give her a potion. Instead, she practically assaulted her with a healing spell. As a testament to the high elf's emotional state, she used too much Mind, and the jade magic glow healed Aiz's wounds in an instant, even restoring her stamina.

"You went to the Dungeon by yourself?! How much were you fighting?! No, *what* were you fighting?!"

"...Infant dragons."

Infant dragons.

A rare monster that appeared on the eleventh and twelfth floors, it was the only dragon in the upper floors—the monster that held the greatest potential. For the upper-floor region that didn't have Monster Rexes, it was effectively the floor boss.

Hearing the name of that monster from Aiz's mouth, Riveria felt her shock give way to rage.

"I beat it, but…but it's still *not enough*…I have to beat more."

Meeting the elf's eyes with her emotionless gaze, Aiz gradually continued.

Riveria howled at the girl's obsessive level of fighting spirit.

"You fool! Are you out of your mind?! Do you think I'll allow that?!"

"…"

"How many times have I told you never to go to the Dungeon by yourself? Why did you disobey us?!"

"…"

"Why would you do that?!"

She grabbed Aiz's shoulders with both hands, rage and sorrow blending in her voice.

Hanging her head, Aiz gritted her teeth and knocked away the hands that were gripping her shoulders.

"…You wouldn't…"

"Ai…z…?"

"You wouldn't tell me…"

Riveria was in shock as Aiz looked up, glaring at her as she shouted back.

"You wouldn't tell me! You kept quiet about how to level up!"

"!!"

"You tried to hide the part about great feats!"

She shouted at those stunned jade eyes, and her voice became louder as the pent-up anger broke free. She hadn't realized just how angry she was.

"Even though you knew my wish!"

Aiz's feelings couldn't be stopped. Even though she knew that she was making up reasons to hide the truth, she couldn't stop herself from blaming Riveria.

Aiz thought she was getting stronger. That she was growing as they watched over her and she followed their lessons. She thought that they would acknowledge her by now.

But she was wrong.

They wouldn't have faith in her, in her strength. Judging it dangerous, they had hidden the key from her.

If the condition for leveling up had been something else, she wouldn't be so troubled. But for Aiz as she was then, strength was everything. If they couldn't trust her strength, then what value did the War Princess have? She had nothing left to rely on. Their good intentions were a rejection of Aiz's entire being.

Aiz didn't know why it hurt her so much.

But there was no hiding from the fact that the lack of recognition had torn a hole in her heart.

"Where did you hear that…?"

Riveria mumbled in shock—the girl had learned the method to overcome her limits.

Aiz glared, closing her heart off further when the elf didn't deny her accusation.

"I'm going to the Dungeon again. I'm going to go and get my level-up."

Riveria reached out for Aiz, who was clenching the sword in her right hand.

"Calm down and wait, Aiz! This isn't the time for that!"

A wild, emotional swing drove her back.

Smack! Her outstretched hand was knocked away and Aiz pushed her chest. The shocked elf fell back a step as Aiz screamed.

"Then when is the time?!!" she shouted, consumed by her emotions. "I have to become strong! I don't want to waste my time. I can't do that!"

Her mother's smile and her father's words from that day flashed through her head. The scene quickly shattered, and all that remained was a little girl alone in the dark.

It was the piercing wail of a child who could only cry as she drew the sword before her eyes.

"Aiz, listen to me, please. I—"

"No! No! Don't get in my way!" She interrupted Riveria when the elf tried to approach again. Aiz refused to let her get close. "I'm not your doll!"

The next instant—*slap!*

A loud sound came from her cheek. The sword she was gripping slipped to the ground. Staring in shock, Aiz only realized she had been slapped because of the heat emanating from her cheek.

She froze for several seconds. Looking in front of her, she saw the rain-drenched Riveria glaring at her with an expression she had never seen before.

"How dare you. You don't know how I feel, either!"

Part rage, part grief, part suffering.

The raindrops running down her cheeks looked almost like tears to Aiz.

"Do you really not know what I think of you?! Why don't you understand that I—that *we* are worried about you?!"

Riveria's own shout rang out.

It was the first time she had ever showed such a strong reaction. She was a bundle of emotions to rival Aiz's.

The girl's resolve, the determination she had to sacrifice anything, even herself, in order to fulfill her wish, wavered. Pierced by those straightforward jade eyes, her golden eyes faltered, swerved.

"We are...a family."

Aiz was flustered.

That gaze, the pleading.

—But she was also gripped by fury.

At her own stupidity.

At the weak Aiz who had turned her mother and father into memories, who had thrown away her past in order to dive into *now*.

Shock and anger, fear and confusion, all of it swirled inside her.

"Aiz, I lo—"

"Stop it!!"

Aiz screamed.

"No! You're wrong! Don't say that! Don't try to confuse me!"

She kept shouting, "Wrong, wrong," shaking her head violently over and over.

Her doll-like mask slipping, she looked her age: a little girl shaking her hair madly, tossed about on a roiling sea of emotions.

Aiz floundered, trying to deny it. Turning her back on all the memories of Riveria that flashed through her head, she fled into the embrace of her task, shrouded in black flame.

"You're not…"

Aiz's eyes narrowed in fury, glaring at the woman who stood transfixed before her. Opening her quivering lips, she delivered her decisive blow.

"You're not my mother!"

The moment she yelled her rejection of Riveria, it was as if time stopped for both of them. The sounds of the world grew distant. Her scream echoed through the city, quickly drowned out by the sound of the rain.

A rain-soaked silence pierced her ears. Breathing raggedly, Aiz desperately tried to suppress the hiccups rising in her throat.

Why was Aiz hurt when she was the one who had said it?

For some reason, when she saw Riveria's frozen face, she felt an intense regret.

Perhaps because of the falling rain, her field of vision seemed to blur.

"…"

The face of the woman in her golden eyes looked like a *blank mask*. Riveria quietly, emotionlessly responded.

"You are right…I'm not your mother."

"—!!"

"And I can't take her place."

The moment the words left her mouth, Aiz ran off. Turning away from the elf, she picked up the sword she had dropped and kicked the ground with all her might as if trying to destroy it.

Droplets that weren't rain flowed from her eyes. Aiz kept wiping them with her free hand, scattering transparent beads behind her as she ran.

Nothing had changed. Nothing would change.

She had always known that she was alone.

The people who had loved her had left her behind and disappeared. Those blessed days had degraded into long-gone memories, fragments of the past that tormented Aiz.

There was no such thing as eternity. Only the moment. And nothing could soothe that never-ending pain. Loki and the others couldn't do it, and neither could Riveria.

She was alone.

She always had been. And always would be. Always.

Looked down on for being a doll, continuing to kill monsters without ever listening to any voice of reason. Loved by no one, understood by no one.

She should have known that already. Her tears should have long since dried up. And yet, she couldn't rid herself of the feelings clouding her eyes.

She screamed with all her might in an attempt to drown them out, running wildly through the city's darkness.

"..."

Even after the girl had disappeared into the rain, Riveria couldn't move from that spot. How many minutes? Hours? Unable even to chase after that small figure, she stood with the rain pelting down on her.

"Riveria!"

"What of Aiz?! Was she here?"

Voices called out to Riveria as she stood battered by the elements, unmoving and not wearing any rain gear.

Finn and Gareth dashed over to her.

The high elf's lips quivered as she struggled to break her silence.

"Finn...Gareth...What should I do?"

She had never before relied on others for determination, but now she felt helpless, unsure. She didn't know what to do with herself after exchanging barbs with the little girl. Her words were tinged with regret and anguish.

Her comrades from other races held their tongues. They understood just from looking at her after all the times they had fought shoulder to shoulder in the past.

It had been a long time since they had seen Riveria look this frail. In fact, it was probably the first time she had ever seemed so weak.

"What should I do?"

As Finn silently looked at the dispirited elf, Gareth furrowed his brow. Forcefully grabbing the collar of the taller Riveria, he dragged her shocked face closer to his.

"Get a grip, ye damn fool!!"

Gareth's deadly serious, thundering anger shocked Riveria.

"I used to say you elves worry too much! I thought you had gotten better than you used to be, but I see nothin's changed!"

"What'd you say?!"

"If yer gonna act like a teacher or a parent, then have the resolve to do it right!"

Her face suddenly red with anger, Riveria knocked away Gareth's hands. But the dwarf snorted without backing down at all from the fire in her eyes.

"What's that face?"

"What would a dwarf like you know...?! When I'm feeling lost...!"

"Lost? Feh, don't give me that shit!" He continued shouting. "Isn't that lass a lot more lost than you are right now?!"

"!!"

Riveria's eyes widened in shock at his thunderous shout.

"Yer just scared of Aiz! You're tryin' to keep a dignified attitude and pickin' yer words carefully to avoid hurtin' her; you didn't just say how ye feel!"

"..."

"You think ye could tell her with your dithering and beating around the bush?! If ye don't know the right words and ye don't know what to do, then just pull her close and give her a damn hug!"

There was no rebuttal to Gareth's booming voice. Riveria couldn't respond. All she could do was clench her fists.

"Gareth, you went too far."

"…Yeah, I'm sorry. I got a bit too heated."

It's not Riveria's fault; it's all of ours, was what Finn left unsaid. They had all missed the signs that something was wrong with her. Gareth exhaled.

"Riveria, go look for Aiz again. If you aren't there, nothing will change."

"…But she already rejected me. I'm in no place to—"

"*Riveria.*"

This time it was Finn, quietly but forcefully.

"Quit worrying about stupid shit like yer 'place.' Don't belittle the time you've spent by Aiz's side. Or are you saying all of that was a lie?"

This time Riveria hung her head.

"—I thought you were lookin' a bit glum, but I guess none of us've changed." As if having heard their arguments, their patron goddess appeared before them without a care for her drenched body. "Inseparable through thick and thin." She smiled cheerfully.

"Riveria, lift yer head."

"What Aiz needs now isn't our voices."

"Aren't you the one she's been closest to the longest?"

Loki offered encouragement, Finn firm assurance, and Gareth a solid argument. Riveria raised her head and looked back at them.

"Going after the girl who ran away from home is obviously her mama's job."

Half teasing, their patron deity added one last point. Riveria started to argue but couldn't muster the energy and just smiled as she gave in.

Before Finn, Gareth, and Loki found Riveria.

The girl was running through the rain holding her sword.
A deep-purple pair of eyes was watching her.

Inside a building shrouded in darkness, a god smiled.

"Hey, Valletta. You know the Doll Princess?"

"What are you talking about, Thanatos? Of course I know her. She's the little girl Finn and the others are raising. A cheeky rookie who's gotten stronger at a crazy rate…A real piece of work."

The patron gods and the leaders of the Evils were shrouded in darkness. *Thanatos Familia* and several other factions and followers of the evil gods were operating behind the scenes to spread more destruction and upheaval in the city.

"What about her?"

"You see, I happened to lay eyes on her one time, and I've been interested ever since. You can see it smoldering in her eyes even from a distance—that dark-black flame."

Underneath his tattered black hood, the god's eyes were following Aiz. They narrowed as she ran through the city spread out beneath him.

"She's got the scent of death to her, and it's strong. Real strong. Strong enough I can't just leave it alone. I am the God of Death, after all."

Giving off an aura of debauchery, the god Thanatos grinned.

"Hey, Valletta, can we change our plans for today?"

"Huh?"

"Go a little wild, show off, ya know? Make it so *Loki Familia*—anyone who'd get in my way, really—won't come near the Dungeon."

The death god was staring at the golden-haired girl's destination—the city's center, Babel—as he made his proposition.

"I can't order around the gods of other familias. You want to change the plan, then talk to them—"

"It'll be a nice way to mess with *Loki Familia*'s Braver, though…"

"_____"

At the mention of Braver, the Evils leader Valletta Grede fell silent. Finally, as if grasping his divine will, she broke into a smile.

"You pervert. You're after that brat."

"You've got it all wrong. There's no ulterior motive here."

While Valletta turned and spread the new orders to her subordinates,

Thanatos continued watching the girl from behind, his lips twisting to reveal a crescent smile.

"Helping lost children is a god's job, after all."

Aiz proceeded into the Dungeon.

She didn't know why her feet had carried her there. But she had nowhere else left to go, so she headed toward the dark, cold underground labyrinth.

Running, running, always running.

Fleeing from Riveria, she dove into the Dungeon.

Swinging, swinging, always swinging.

Falling into despair, she continued swinging her sword to slaughter all the beasts.

Eyes red and swollen, Aiz kept running. If a monster stood in her path, she put all the violent emotions she was feeling into her Sword Air as she cut through the body. It was fortunate that no one was around. That meant no one could see that even now, she looked ready to cry, and no one could hear her screams verging on childlike sobs. Instead of crying, she kept swinging her sword, surrendering herself to the emotions running wild in her heart.

"Ha…ha…ha…"

Finally, before she could contain those feelings, her body started to give out instead. In her rush, she was barely breathing at all. Her lungs cried out. Her arms and legs were burning up, even to the tips of her fingers and toes. After defeating the last monster standing before her, Aiz stuck her sword into the ground, gasping uncontrollably. She used it as a staff for a while.

Finally peeling her cheek off the tip of the hilt, she looked up.

"This is…the twelfth floor?"

A white haze drifted around her. The floor was covered in a light fog like the kind that fell early in the morning. There were countless bare trees that turned into nature weapons growing all around.

Judging from the size of the room and the fact that she recognized the lay of the land, Aiz could guess where she was.

The place she had reached in her haphazard running was the deepest room in the lowest floor of the Dungeon's upper-level region.

"...I..."

You belong here.

When the other Aiz dwelling in her heart—when the dark flame seemed to whisper that in her ear, she wrapped her arms around herself.

—I want to become strong. Stronger than anything. So I never have to lose anything.

—I'm scared. I'm lonely. I'm cold. I'm always alone. There's nothing left for me. I'm sad.

The two voices contradicted each other. They were both hers. Looking steadily ahead, the flame in her eyes flared up.

In the empty room with no more traces of monsters, Aiz was desperately struggling against the feelings welling up inside her.

"—Is it painful, o lost child?"

"!"

A solemn yet seductive voice reverberated, caressing her ears. Gasping, Aiz swung back around. A single shadow rose from the white mist.

A black-robed person. The dark-purple hair that fell from the deep hood was long like a woman's, and the body was slender. The perfect features of the newcomer's face were bewitching. More than anything, this being's licentious aura was like nothing Aiz had felt before.

...A god?

Judging from his handsome demeanor and the otherworldly atmosphere, she felt suspicious. That should have marked him as a god, but for some reason, the feeling she got from him was different. As if he was missing one of the pieces that would mark his divinity. She was perplexed.

She had no way of knowing that he was suppressing his divine will in order to enter the Dungeon. Thanatos smiled suspiciously. As he approached, several shadows appeared behind him, as if to defend him. Seeing the robed figures, Aiz gasped.

Could it be...the Evils?

Aiz was on guard against this god. His very presence in the Dungeon made this an unheard-of situation. Unsure what he was after, she started to ready her sword.

"Do you hate monsters, little girl?"

"!"

Shock colored her face.

"You can't forgive your own weakness…Your heart has been led astray by the world that has allowed you to remain weak…"

"…!"

Aiz was shaken, and he continued to confound her with his words and that bewitching smile.

"You're feeling trapped, conflicted, in the grips of an impulse tearing you apart. You are an apostle of revenge seeking power…A pure swordswoman starving for strength. Your heart will never be healed…You don't know the method for containing that black flame of destruction hidden inside you."

He spoke Aiz's fears and thoughts without any hesitation. She recoiled. The god's beautiful voice had a wondrous tone to it that bewitched mortals. Even if she wanted to close her ears, she couldn't. Like magic.

"No one understands you…You are alone."

At those words, Aiz's face finally cracked.

"You hate it, don't you? You're sad, aren't you? You're anxious, aren't you?"

And as the girl's face changed, Thanatos's purple eyes, which resembled an abyss shining from beneath his hood, narrowed.

"Shall I release you from your suffering?"

"!!"

Her golden eyes wavered.

"Child, you are beautiful. I think one who has fallen in love with death as she fights and fights is a lovely thing. I want to save you."

"…?!"

"I shall give you power. The ability to get stronger, a place where you can fulfill your wish. A place where you don't have to be lost. The world of swords and flame you desire.

"It's also a way to escape your current slump, a place to fight you will never tire of, a relief to allow you to escape this suffering."

Aiz's heart trembled at the sweet refrain of his voice. The black flame roared in delight. It begged to be released from the constricting embrace of *Loki Familia* to continue moving forward.

Free us from the pain of loneliness—just worry about getting stronger, it pleaded.

"Entrust yourself to the flames blazing in your eyes. If you do, the world around you will change. It will bless you."

The god's prayer tempted the child's heart. It was salvation from the heavens as well as a step onto the path to destruction. A cursed ritual to give birth to a murderous angel spreading untold death for his benefit.

Thanatos opened his eyes wide and reached out his hand to the fledgling swordswoman of death he sensed in her.

"Come with me. Everything you desire, I can grant you."

Aiz looked at the beautiful god's hand.

It represented relief from all her suffering. A path of carnage seeking the power she desired without any other concerns. The entrance to the world she should have wanted more than anything.

I...

Her vision warped, and the god's hand changed shape.

It morphed into the place that Aiz needed to reach, the summit of a mountain of monster corpses and the enormous objective beyond that.

I'm always alone. If I can't change that, then I'd rather not feel anything. I don't care how dirty my hands get or what others think—I can just be a child who lusts for power. The black flame raged in her heart, and a heat strong enough to burn spread across her back, stirring her up.

Finally the girl's hand trembled, as if to loosen its grip on her sword. Just as she was about to be swallowed by the black flame and surrender herself to her desires…

A single high elf's gaze appeared in her mind.

―――

The look on her face when they had last parted, a visage warped by a familiar suffering. Aiz's memories of the time with her until now, of the people who had watched over her, resurfaced in her heart. Her trusted sword flashed, catching her eye as if calling out to her.

She didn't know why she remembered that now.

She didn't know why she couldn't let go of the sword.

But no matter how she tried, Aiz couldn't reject everything that had happened.

The days she spent with them—sometimes stormy, sometimes peaceful—replaced the black flame like a wind blowing through the sky...

"...I want power."

Time began to move again as her lips trembled. As she looked into Thanatos's eyes, the black flame receded from her golden eyes, and the swordlike gleam returned.

"But joining you...is wrong!"

Resolutely, she turned down the god's invitation.

"Even if I end up alone...betraying them...would be wrong!"

As she shouted her thoughts, Aiz changed. She glared at the god.

What stood before her was a symbol of darkness, clad in black robes. As if an illusion had shattered, the God of Evil's smile looked repulsive as he held out his hand. Once the internal discord clouding her eyes had cleared, she saw through him.

Thanatos stopped smiling, going silent. But after a few moments, he shrugged.

"—Toooo bad."

Losing his godly splendor and the enchanting visage, a single shallow god was what emerged. Thanatos smiled flippantly as Aiz doubted her eyes.

"And I thought I was gonna win over the rumored Doll Princess... If you could have developed some, you would have sent who knows how many people to the heavens as one of the followers of my beloved Death."

"…?!"

"Man, I really screwed this up. You were a lot stronger than I thought you'd be."

As Thanatos revealed his true self, a chill ran up Aiz's spine. The atmosphere changed, but his degenerate nature hadn't changed a bit.

She was afraid of this shallow being and the traces of madness his words revealed.

This was an evil god, like the ones Loki and Finn and the others had mentioned. She was sure of it.

"Who are you?!"

"I'd love to tell you more about myself, but I can't now that you've turned me down. The Evils can be suuuch a pain."

Pulling his hood up to hide his eyes, Thanatos curled his lips, smiling back at Aiz.

"Well then…Unfortunately, I promised Valletta I'd clean up the loose ends if the invitation was rejected…"

At the phrase *clean up the loose ends*, Aiz immediately readied her sword. The Evils followers who had accompanied Thanatos as bodyguards moved out. The two warriors who had hidden in the fog shifted to block her way.

Two on one…Can I win?

Despite all the practice fights she had had with Finn and Gareth, she didn't have any real experience in an actual fight against another person. She was unsure whether she would shrink from a deadly exchange of shouts and flying blood or be able to stand her ground, but Finn and Gareth had far more of a presence. They were probably lower-level adventurers like her. If that was the case, she thought she had a chance to win.

However, ignoring Aiz's calculations, Thanatos spoke as if he was a world apart from them.

"Ah, I just thought of something interesting."

Recalling a child's playfulness, he snapped his fingers.

Beneath his hood, his lips revealed a cool crescent.

"Little Doll Princess, let me give you a present."

"…?"

"I've always wanted to try this once."

Aiz looked at Thanatos suspiciously. Even the Evils with him seem flustered as they glanced at him as he raised a single arm over his head.

Touching the bedrock ceiling, he smiled as his deep-purple eyes narrowed.

"Just for you."

The next instant, he unleashed the divine will he had been suppressing.

"—?!"

A dark-purple swirl was visible—the God of Death's *color*—turning into a small column of light as it pierced the labyrinth's ceiling.

Immediately after, *that* arrived.

The first thing that occurred was an earthquake.

As if moaning, or undulating, or angry, the labyrinth's floor rumbled.

While Aiz gazed in wonder at the unknown, having never experienced anything like this in all the time she had been coming to the labyrinth, the walls began to howl. From three points buried in the white mist—where the exits were—she heard the thunder of a rockslide.

It can't be—the exits are blocked?!

The instinctual analysis of the situation that flashed through Aiz's head left her dumbfounded. The Evils followers had the same reaction.

Thanatos paid them no mind; his smile remained unchanged. The god, who was comfortably accepting the unceasing tremors assaulting them, all of a sudden looked up.

"Ahhh—this is what happens."

Aiz looked up as well, and just as she did, *crumble.*

"_____"

Cracks formed in the labyrinth's ceiling.

Fragments rained down, and she laid eyes on the *thing* the Dungeon was summoning.

Aiz's eyes froze over.

At the same time.

"—"

In the Guild's underground temple, the old god groaned.

"Ouranos?"

"...A god has trespassed in the Dungeon."

He furrowed his brow deeply as he answered the question from his black-robed follower.

"Freya..."

"...I'd like to stop it. But making more trouble is..."

They were in the giant white tower.

"It really shook there, my goddess...My goddess?"

"Which dumbass unleashed that...?"

And on Main Street lined with weapon shops.

"Hey, hey...This is way past playing with fire."

"Hermes, what happened?"

And in a manor far from the center of the city.

"Ganesha! It's the Evils. They've struck a magic-stone factory in the northeast!"

"...Got it. Get going, all of you!"

And in a part of town where the military police were gathered.

All the gods in Orario felt it and understood what it was. Because it was unleashed in the upper floors close to the ground, there was no mistaking it.

And of course, *they* also felt it.

"Oi, Loki, what was that?"

"This timing is too perfect..."

Loki stared suspiciously at the ground as the quivering died down. Her response to Gareth's question hung in the air.

"Captain! The Evils have appeared! It seems they're attacking the Industrial District, and *Ganesha Familia* is requesting immediate support!"

One of *Loki Familia*'s members appeared, bearing an emergency report.

"What? At a time like this? Finn!"

"…Yeah, let's go. We can't just abandon the Industrial District."

For Orario, which boasted the only magic-stone industry in the world, the Industrial District that produced them was the city's economic heart. If that was destroyed, it would be a huge blow to the Labyrinth City.

Finn bit his thumb as he glanced over at Loki before unleashing a flurry of orders.

"Gareth, get a squad of the fastest people and head out first. I'll take the overall command."

"Aye!"

"Give the order for everyone to move out!"

"Understood!"

Gareth and the messenger ran off. About to follow after them, Finn swung around to face Riveria.

"Finn…I…"

"Riveria, you search for Aiz."

"!"

"I've got a bad feeling about this. Make sure you bring her back. You have to go get her!"

The prum leader immediately dashed after them, leaving the high elf with that order as he disappeared into the rain.

Riveria snapped out of her reverie when Loki grabbed one of her arms.

"The Dungeon."

"?"

"Aiz is definitely in the Dungeon. No, there's no place else she could be. Somethin' stinks." Loki grabbed Riveria's shoulders, her face tense as rain dripped from her crimson hair. "If my instincts are right, Aiz's in a reeeal bad spot right now."

"…!"

"Go, Riveria. Ya don't have time to be hesitatin'. Go help her."

You're the only one who can.

Riveria could see the unspoken words in Loki's wide crimson eyes. Silently…she clenched her fist in determination.

The patron goddess smiled as the elf nodded.

"Sorry, Loki. I'll be back."

Having made up her mind, Riveria started running.

She headed for the city's center, toward the white tower rising in the darkness.

A shower of debris fell as *it* was born in the labyrinth.

Sharp claws, long fangs, innumerable scales, and distorted, filmy wings.

Its entire body was jet-black.

Aiz's heart screamed at the upside-down thing emerging from the ceiling. As it raised its head.

That's.

That's.

That's…!

She forcefully gripped the sword's hilt. Her heart felt like it was going to beat out of her chest, or maybe even burst.

Ignoring Aiz, who was fixated on *that*, Thanatos pulled out a silver orb that looked like a magic item from his breast pocket.

"Well then, Doll Princess, have fun. I'll be leaving before I get torn to pieces."

Without even glancing at the thing on the ceiling, he turned away like an uninterested bystander. Taking the trembling, scared, panicking Evils followers with him, he headed deeper into the mist.

"You'll have to return to the heavens one step ahead of me—my beloved girl."

His black-robed figure disappeared into the fog with those parting words.

The jet-black creatured fully emerged from the broken bedrock, falling from the ceiling and spreading its wings. It rose in the air with a great screech.

"—*Ooooooooooooooooooooooooooo!!*"

The creature unleashed a scream that made even the mist in the room tremble.

Her eardrums quivering from the monster's roar, Aiz forgot to even cover her ears as the image of the intruder was seared into her eyes.

It was a dragon.

It should have been impossible for a true dragon to appear on the upper floors. And yet, here was one with wings.

A wyvern.

A monster that inhabited the middle-floor region. From its long outstretched tail to its head, it was more than five meders long. Despite being shrouded in fog, there was no mistaking that it was a species of dragon. Wyverns' bodies were usually a pale-red color, but the tough scales covering this one were pure black. It was clearly an Irregular, a subspecies hiding far more strength than the usual.

A black dragon.

While Aiz stared, unmoving, it spread its wings far above her head, its red eyes surveying the floor below. It seemed to be glaring at the veil of mist blocking its view as it opened its mouth, baring the rows of fangs in its jaws.

A ball of flame sparkled in the back of its mouth, glowing brighter.

Aiz's eyes opened as far as they could.

And then...

"———————————!"

It unleashed a flame breath. The river of fire hit the ground beneath it with a thunderous explosion, kicking up dirt as it rocked the ground. The dragon swung its head as the brutal crimson light streamed from its mouth. An unceasing eruption of flame poured down, following its head all around the room.

"———?!"

Aiz ran with all her might to escape the waves of flame surrounding her. She jumped behind a small hill to get any cover she could, just barely escaping the blazing hot ball of flame that passed over where she'd stood a moment ago.

"Oooo..."

The intense flame breath blew away all the room's mist.

Evaporated it.

Under the cover of the hill, she reeled to her feet, taken aback at the scene unfolding.

Bare trees and grassland turned to a blazing hellscape. A big tree, its trunk carbonized, crashed to the ground. The misty floor had turned to scorched earth as sparks flew everywhere.

Flashes of flame escaping the gaps in its fangs, the wyvern swung its head around, puzzled.

Because its intended target was not visible in the red glow lighting its field of view. Thanatos and his followers, who should have been hidden in the mists, had suddenly vanished, despite the exits still being blocked. The apostle of destruction born of the will of the Dungeon wavered, its target having escaped *outside the Dungeon* by some as-yet-unknown way.

Before long, though, by process of elimination, the dragon's eyes lit upon the sole remaining prey—Aiz.

"OOOOOOOOoooo!"

"?!"

Her golden eyes wavered as the dragon dropped from the ceiling. Its commanding presence was more fiendish than that of any monster Aiz had ever faced. There was no choice but to run. Its menacing howl made the girl's skin crawl.

However, Aiz gripped her sword with all her strength. A tremendous fighting spirit overwhelmed that small fear. Emotion rocked her body as she put aside everything leading up to that moment.

Facing the wyvern flying at her, Aiz sprinted.

"Uwaaaaaaa!"

Even she didn't know where the ferocity came from. The young girl roared as she raised her trusted Sword Air aloft. Facing the wyvern that grew bigger and bigger as it drew closer, she let loose with a sharp slash.

"!"

"Gu?!"

As they passed each other, Aiz was knocked to the scorched earth by the absurdly powerful shock wave of the charge. Despite just barely dodging its claws, she still felt the force of it tearing at her. Immediately peeling herself off the ground, she tracked the shadow dancing back into the sky.

On the other hand, the wyvern glanced disinterestedly at its body. A single scale had been broken on its shoulder near the base of its great wings. Even if it was just a small chink, the dragon's defense that should have withstood any attack had been broken. The wyvern glared back at the undersized little girl beneath it who was fixing it with a sharp gaze.

It commenced its descent again, looking down with murderous intent at the blade shining blue and sharp.

"—!"

Aiz kicked the ground. Her aim was a boulder about as tall as she was. Using the momentum of her sprint, she spun just before she reached the boulder protruding out of the grassland and swung her Sword Air with all her might.

As the wyvern flew in from above, she hit it with the fragments of the rock.

"!"

The strengthened Damascus blade shattered the boulder spectacularly, sending countless pieces flying in a ranged attack when the dragon was least expecting it. It could only regret its speed as it bore the full brunt of the attack head-on.

Gagagaga! She could hear the hard blows landing one after the other.

The wyvern had immediately averted its eyes to avoid the fragments of stone, slowing down just the slightest bit. Clad in dragon scales, it didn't receive a single wound, but its field of view was blocked.

Aiz seized that moment.

The theory for beating winged monsters is—

She quickly leaped. Shock registered in the dragon's eyes as the little girl got above it.

Aim for the wings—knock them down to the ground!

Eyes flashing, Aiz unleashed the strongest sword technique she could.

"GUOOOOOO?!"

The rippled steel blade carved into the dragon's wing, sending red drops of blood flying.

The attack with all her might pierced the dragon scales, reaching the meat below its defenses.

It was a technique. The sword technique that had so totally shocked Loki and Finn—the special move of a certain man from her memories. The crispness of that tremendous technique managed to overcome the vast difference in Status and leave a wound on the dragon.

Subconsciously, Aiz had drawn out all of herself. Finn's, Gareth's, and Riveria's teachings, as well as the swordsmanship of the hero she had always watched as a child.

Before an enemy she needed to defeat, all the pieces of her that she had gained before now moved as one in order to knock it down.

That was still shallow!—It's not over yet!

Off-balance, the wyvern was forced to land. Hitting the ground a second later, Aiz didn't wait a moment to continue her assault. Her target was its wing. Cut off its means of flight. Ignoring its howl of rage, she struck it with a flash of steel.

Consumed by an inferno of emotions, Aiz lashed out with sword techniques that contained her whole being. Vestiges of her father that she hadn't yet grasped, the remnants left behind for her. She used those techniques to just barely dodge the enemy's flailing teeth and claws as her battle clothes were torn to pieces.

From the side, from the back, she kept moving, swinging her sword from outside the enemy's field of view. With each flash, fragments of scales scattered, and neither she nor her enemy could tell whose fresh blood was spilled with each clash.

The girl raged as if possessed.

"—*Uuuuu.*"

However.

That only incurred the dragon's wrath.

The wyvern's eyes flashed at the tiny beast who kept biting at it constantly, not recognizing the difference of level between their species.

Once Aiz leaped, aiming for its wings, it forcefully turned its body. Its scaly tail swung around, knocking away everything that approached.

"Ahhh?!"

The tail hit Aiz directly in the chest.

Wrapped in hardened scales, it was a fiendish bludgeon no weaker than an adventurer's high-level weapon. Aiz coughed up blood, struck with a force equivalent to a giant club. Despite immediately putting her sword in front of herself to block, her armor plates were crushed, stripped off of her, and blown away by the dreadful force...

"*Gaaa~~~~~~?!*"

Thanks to the protection of the Damascus sword, she had just barely avoided an instant death, but she was damaged unlike anything she had experienced before. Cracks started to form in her trusted sword. She coughed up blood as she writhed in agony on the ground.

Ignoring her suffering, the wyvern easily flew into the air. Its eyes flashed dangerously as it glared down at the floor of the Dungeon. Burning with rage, it decided to use its greatest weapon, opening its mouth.

"*AAAAaa!*"

"!!"

Its deadly breath poured onto the earth.

With a power several times that of the fireballs a standard wyvern could breathe, it assaulted Aiz with a savage, hellish rain. She hit the ground with her fists, desperately trying to escape as she rolled away from it, but the scale of the attack was not something a lower-tier adventurer could hope to resist.

Finally.

"—…?! The flames…"

Lifting her head, Aiz was surrounded by a wall of fire.

The scene of purgatory had perfectly cut off all means of retreat. She had nowhere to run. The wyvern would have no mercy on the human who had wounded it. The wyvern, king of beasts, looked down upon all that existed below it, unleashing a cruel crimson flash to turn everything to ash.

"*OOOOOUU!!*"

It was a giant fireball, more than five meders wide.

Aiz's world shone red as she looked up in horror.

"~~~~~~~~~~~~?!"

The world was tinged red.

She exhausted the last little bit of her strength to avoid a direct hit, but inside the wall of flames, the waves of heat and shock buffeted Aiz. In an instant, the armor on her body melted.

The whirling inferno scoffed at her futile struggle to resist with all her might as her skin and hair were scorched. Merely by exhaling, the wyvern's frighteningly hot breath pushed her down.

"*Aaaaaaaaaaa…?!*"

Sticking her sword into the ground, desperately trying to stand, she couldn't even control her breathing. Her throat and lungs were starting to burn, and she couldn't move from her kneeling position. The room had been turned into hell's furnace, threatening to incinerate the girl.

I…

Aiz could hear her body being singed. The hopeless sound of sparks falling and burning her arms and legs.

Am I…going to die here?

I won't…

I won't allow it. You haven't done anything yet. Stand up. Take your sword. Howl! Turn it all into hatred and strike down that dragon. Fulfill my wish!

Aiz's heart cried out. She tried to stand up.

My back is hot.

My back is hot.

The black flame was flaring up.

The flame in her eyes tried to push her to struggle.

But.

Even the font of that black flame was on the verge of being burned out by the enemy's inferno. The enemy's flame was hotter. Hot enough to burn away Aiz's worst resolve and leave no traces.

Is this...?

The brutal waves of heat were obscuring her consciousness. Her sense of time slowed in the red world. Aiz's consciousness started to fade away at the same moment her trusted sword started to melt.

It will all be easier now—a voice of despair and hopelessness that had always lurked in her whispered.

No! I refuse!—The black flame tried to resist with all its might.

But it's already...—Her roasting body started to give in.

In the end, nothing had changed.

Nothing had been achieved.

Aiz would die alone, consumed by flames.

What a stupid death. What a disappointing demise. What a sad ending.

As the voices in her heart melted, Aiz lifted her head.

The wyvern was slowly opening its mouth. It was preparing to deliver the finishing blow. A giant fireball to scorch the entire floor and Aiz with it.

Aiz's mind turned to white as she was unable to even stand, about to be swallowed up by the bright flames.

"Aiz!"

One of the entrances to the room blew open with an explosion, and she heard someone calling her name.

"_____"

The moment she recognized the high elf Riveria, time stopped.

An inexplicable emotion rushed through her in an instant, completely different from the despair that had filled her before. A light shone on the girl cowering in the darkness, a jade glow pressing against her chest.

Following the monsters drawn by the God of Death's divine will, Riveria had found this location. She had blasted away the barrier at the entrance using magic. The moment she set foot in the room that had transformed into a furnace—she lost her voice seeing the girl trapped in a cage of flames.

The wyvern mercilessly unleashed its giant fireball at the little girl.

"Aiz! Say it! Call it forth!!"

Before Aiz could be engulfed by the inferno, Riveria shouted. As the crimson flame approached the burning Aiz, she heard those words.

"Awaken, Tempest!"

And the instant before the fireball burst, Aiz's mouth formed the same sound.

"Awaken, Tempest!"

The magic inside Aiz was unleashed.

"—!"

"?!"

A giant explosion rocketed upward. A resounding magic felt by Riveria and the wyvern. The giant fireball landed, exploding into fragments, bringing the scene to light.

Despite what should have been a direct hit, the girl hadn't been turned to ash.

"This is…"

Kneeling on the ground, Aiz was protected by the wind.

The torrent swirled around her little body. A wind armor stronger, more elegant, more sublime than any other. It was Aiz's magic that was engraved deep within her body. The divine protection of wind, watching over the lonely girl.

"Ah—"

Aiz knew what the wind embracing and dancing around her body was without any explanation.

"Mother's…wind."

The wind Aiz had always seen when she was younger.

"…Always."

She had always felt it, her mother's gentle breath.

"…She'll always…be with me…!"

The spirit of wind had never left her side.

"_____!!"

Power welled up inside her, overflowing. And with it came memories and tears that left her trembling. Bracing herself on her knees, she heard the wind's voice grow louder, as if supporting Aiz while she tried to stand.

"…?!"

The wyvern shuddered, clearly shaken by the wild wind swirling beneath it.

A wind pressure strong enough to defend against its fireball.

A magic strong enough to faze even a dragon. Without regard for its appearance, the dragon that had lost its kingly demeanor prepared to roast the girl again. Gathering the next giant round in its mouth, it gave off a crimson gleam.

"Fuuu—!!"

Aiz didn't let that opportunity escape her. Unleashing the full strength of the wind her body had been given, she turned into the eye of a ferocious storm. A whirlwind so strong that Riveria had to cover her face with her arm as the shimmering cage of flame enclosing the girl was blown away.

And then she rode the wind.

"?!"

The wind armor launched her forward at an incredible speed to bring her below the wyvern.

While the monster lost sight of her, Aiz dashed up one of the trees still standing in a single leap and kicked off a branch with the next step, taking flight.

Borrowing the power of wind, Aiz turned into a tornado arrow.

"Uaaaaaaaaaaaaaaaaaaaaaaaaa!"

The giant fireball the wyvern was building backfired. Because it was charging a powerful attack, it couldn't move. Defense, evasion, preemptive attack—all were impossible. Thanks to her quick judgment and the wind, Aiz closed in with a speed that betrayed all the dragon's expectations.

The dragon's eyes were bloodshot with unease; the red light emanating from its mouth shone brighter and grew larger.

As Aiz roared, the trusted sword in her hands was enveloped in the flowing wind.

Her back was hot.

Her back was burning.

The black blaze was flaring in anticipation of striking it down.

However, more than that.

The wind embracing Aiz raged.

As if protecting the girl, as if embracing its child.

It will be okay, it seemed to whisper.

Tears scattering in the wind, Aiz swung the sword with all her power and gave birth to a maelstrom.

"—OOOOOOOOOOOOOOOOOO?!"

The gap between them disappeared. The wyvern had just finished charging its fire breath, preparing to unleash it. Before the flaring mass of fire could go off—

Aiz swung her sword of wind down.

"Airiel!!"

The storm broke.

"―――――――――*Aaaaaa?!*"

The sword swung at the dragon's head and unleashed the wind.

The giant tornado blew away the creature's mouth and upper jaw. With nowhere to go, the stream of flames backfired in a giant explosion.

"Aiz?!"

Riveria screamed at the thunderous explosion blooming above her head, scorching the floor's ceiling, and leaving cracks in the bedrock. The girl's body broke through the black smoke and sparks, falling to the ground.

Somehow controlling her magic, fragments of wind scattering

around her, Aiz landed on the ground. Shaken badly by the impact, she looked about to collapse but just managed to stay on her feet. While Riveria rushed to her side, Aiz dropped her sword to the ground, as if her hands were declaring they had had enough.

However, the wind still embraced the girl's body.

"Ah...Ahhhhh...—"

Looking down at her hands as the wind caressed her, embraced her shoulders, Aiz couldn't stop crying.

She had thought there was nothing left for her.

She had imagined that she was always alone.

She was sure an eternity of pain and suffering awaited her.

But she was wrong.

Her mother's breath, their connection, still remained.

It was inside her, always holding her close.

The sword at her feet shone, teaching her what she hadn't realized.

Her father's sword techniques lived on in Aiz.

Her mother's wind resided with Aiz.

"W-waaaaaa...!"

I...

I wasn't...

I wasn't alone.

"Aiz..."

Unable to contain her sobbing, Aiz turned around. Riveria stood before her eyes.

That gaze had always been trying to tell her what she had just realized.

You aren't alone.

Filled with regret as she looked at the girl covered in wounds, those moist jade eyes revealed the love that was hidden behind them.

"Aiz...I can't be your mother...but...I want to be by your side."

Tears flowed down her cheeks.

"I love you."

As the traces of her mother overlapped with Riveria, this time Aiz didn't reject her. Hands gently reached behind her shoulders, wrapping her in a warm embrace. The warmth of those hands summoned more tears to Aiz's eyes. Pressing her face into Riveria's stomach, the tears that she thought had dried up flowed out.

"Riveriaaa, R-Riveriaaa…! I'm so sorryyyy!"

"It's okay. It's okay…It'll be okay…"

As her overwhelming sobs got in the way, interrupting Aiz's apology, Riveria smiled through her own tears, unable to speak clearly herself.

Instead, she just tightened her hold, bringing the girl closer.

Aiz wailed, crying even harder.

In the middle of the scorched earth, two figures overlapped.

The girl's sobs echoed through the room, reaching the ears of the fairies and evoking their sympathy. The remnants of her magic turned into a gentle wind, wrapping around the two of them.

As if smiling at them, as if calming them, the wind embraced the mother and child.

"…You know, Bell, gods and children might not be able to live out the same lives."

What is an eternal love?

Aiz asked no one in particular as she heard the goddess's voice.

"But I will always be by your side."

Kam died.

His beloved children—his family unrelated by blood at his side, in tears.

"Even if death forces us apart…I *will* come find you."

He had always been plagued by regret and feelings of remorse, but in the end, he had been saved.

Because of the memories of his goddess living on inside him.

Hestia had revived the bond with his love, Brigit.

Even in his loss, an *eternity* that could soothe his loneliness existed within Kam.

It was something that had probably never stopped haunting him, but in his final moments, he was saved by what remained of that goddess and passed in peace.

"No matter how many hundreds, thousands, millions of years it takes, I will find you after your rebirth…"

Her bond with Kam would live on forever in the goddess's memories.

"And when I find you, I'll say, 'Would you join my familia?'"

Just like Hestia was saying now.

"—Ah."

The sobbing Bell had struggled to contain broke through and grew louder until they reached Aiz's ears.

They were in the dark forest, where he had fled after seeing Kam's death. Scared of the eternal suffering brought by loss, he was crying, cradled by Hestia as she spoke.

"I'm not the only one. Other gods' and goddesses' bonds with children like you can last forever."

A modest vow of an eternal love, just like the one she had sworn.

"After all, we are gods. We live forever, you know."

Leaning her back against a tree trunk near them, Aiz heard those words.

They weren't unchanging, like Hestia and the other gods.

They would lose everything eventually.

Eternity did not exist for them.

However—

There would be things left behind.

There were bonds that would last a lifetime after they passed.

Whether in memories, or warmth, or thoughts.

Like the wind residing in Aiz's breast.

Like the pattern of her father's sword that was engraved in her hands.

The things her parents left behind still lived on in Aiz.

"Goddess…I want to always, always be with you…!"

"Yes…"

Behind Aiz, the boy's tears fell.

"I will always be with you, Bell."

His teary voice rang out as she held him to her chest.

Aiz averted her eyes before softly raising her head.

"Always…together…"

The boy's thoughts and the goddess's words came to her lips.

She felt like the wind residing within her was embracing her now.

"Mother…"

She whispered as she gazed beyond the woods' canopy to the golden moon in the dark night sky.

Putting her hand on her breast, Aiz gazed up with a strong determination at the sky that spread out before her. The sky that connected the ends of the Earth.

"Wait for me…"

She made a vow to the wind that had been left for her, to the eternal bond living on in her heart.

"I swear…I will take you back."

THE
MOMENT
THAT THE
WIND
WISHED
FOR

Гэта казка іншага свету

◆

Цяпер, калі хацеў вецер

The eastern sky started to grow bright.

The fog started to clear, and the early-morning air was crisp. The rain clouds had moved away, and birdcalls echoed in the forest.

Aiz, Bell, and the goddess they had recovered stood in front of Edas Village.

"Lady Hestia, Mr. Bell, please come again anytime."

"Thank you, Miss Rina. I'd be glad to."

"Thanks, Rina, and everyone from the village. I won't forget what you did for us."

"That goes for us, too. Father found peace because you guys came."

Her eyes still red from crying, Rina smiled at the two of them.

In the end, they had stayed one more day after the festival in order to help with Kam's burial and offer a prayer for his happiness in the next life.

On the fifth day after the incident in the Beor Mountains, all the villagers conveyed their thanks, starting with Rina.

"Miss Aiz, too—let's meet again…!"

"Yes…let's."

Taking the teary Rina's hand, Aiz flashed a small smile.

She promised to meet her friend from the outside world again.

After a little while, they set out from the village, watched over by the large group of villagers who had gathered despite the early hour.

The sun started to show its face over the eastern ridge, shining on the maze of valleys and forests. They escaped the sea of trees and crossed through a gap in a precipice, listening to the river's now peaceful burble as they descended the Beor Mountains.

"That was a nice place, wasn't it…?"

"Wouldn't it be great to visit them again?"

"…If you go, I want to come with…"

"Huh? Are…are you sure that's okay?!"

"Yes."

"H-hey, hold on a second there, Wallensomething! Don't make promises out of the blue! If you want to go, go with your own familia!"

As she spoke with them, she smiled.

Looking at them from the side, they seemed refreshed. What had happened in that village had left several different emotions in her heart, but she felt like it had shown her something as well.

That's what Aiz thought as those images from her memory remained in her heart.

Let's go back—

To where everyone is waiting.

To the woman who said she loved me.

Having traveled away from the city, through a bit of the outside world now, there were so many things she wanted to say.

Aiz continued down the mountain path to the city, her eyes twinkling as she saw the giant white tower jutting high into the sky beyond the southern ridge.

A transparent blue sky stretched out into the distance.

Orario's sky was so clear that it made the pouring rain just the other day seem like it had never been. Beneath that azure sky were the sounds of wagon wheels and haggling shoppers and the playful laughter of innocent children at play.

"That dumbass Ares was already caught in the mountains and dragged to Guild Headquarters. Their god was captured, so this pain-in-the-ass war should finally be over now."

"It's because we sent so many adventurers into the Beor Mountains. We managed to pin down their exact location. Perseus, who got called in for support, will probably get a special award."

"Would've been nice to bring Aiz and those two back as part of the bargain."

The peaceful, everyday bustle of Orario came in through the window.

They were in the office in *Loki Familia*'s home, the Twilight Manor.

The leadership group and Loki were mainly discussing the resolution of the war with the kingdom. Listening to the current situation, Finn looked up.

He glanced over at the high elf, who was standing there without speaking.

"Riveria?"

"Hmm…Ah, sorry. Go ahead."

"You worried about Aiz?"

"…Aiz isn't a child anymore. Worrying about her is a waste of time."

She responded as if she was surprised by the silliness of the question.

"You've sure seemed lost in thought for a while now, though."

"Riveria's been spacin' out a lot lately when she's by herself, too."

"Don't be silly."

The dwarf and goddess grinned at each other when she glared at them.

"There's no need to hide it. If it had been five days with no news from us, you'd be worried, too."

"My number of Blessings hasn't gone down, so I can at least be sure she's alive."

"She runs away from home all the time, but it's the first time she's left the city. Even if ye try to ignore your parental instincts, it isn't that strange."

Riveria sullenly glared as her old friends said what they wanted.

But she didn't try to deny what they were saying. A sigh passed her small lips as she subconsciously fiddled with her golden hair band.

"…From time to time, I become dreadfully anxious. I start to wonder whether those black flames that still lurk inside her might consume her at any moment. Whether they might take her someplace far away."

"…"

"Aiz has grown, and now she's one of our core members. The familia's gotten bigger. We should give her some room to stand on her own. I can hear myself saying it, but…even so. I am still always watching over her."

As Riveria quietly opened her heart, they listened in silence.

You're not alone. Riveria had let Aiz know, but she wondered if really she wanted to hear it herself.

She smiled awkwardly, though not quite self-deprecatingly.

"Even just not seeing her for a little while like this, the uneasiness grows."

"That's just part of bein' a mother. Nothin' wrong with it."

"Who are you calling a mother?" Riveria smiled as she turned to Loki.

"—Captain! Captain!!"

Raul burst through the door and into the office without knocking.

"Aiz's back! Just now she came in the north gate and is headed here!"

Before Finn and the others could open their mouths, even before Raul could finish speaking, her jade hair moved.

Raul was surprised as Riveria passed him and left the room. The others glanced at one another, holding in a chuckle.

She passed through the long hallway and down the stairs to the main entrance.

There, bathed in a bright light, was a crowd of familia members and a golden-haired, golden-eyed girl greeting them.

"Miss Aiz! I was so worried!"

"Ah, Aiz made her cry."

"Lefiya was really worried without you."

"I'm sorry…Lefiya."

"Feh, there wasn't any damn reason to be worried about her."

"That's rich coming from you, Bete. Your tail was fidgeting the whole time~."

"It was not!! Quit spouting crap, you stupid Amazon!"

"What'd you say?!"

Riveria's eyes softened at the heartwarming scene and happy voices. That small, beaten-up, lonely little girl was long gone. She was able to smile and had found a place to come home to.

That gave her peace of mind and a kind of happiness that she would hold close to her heart.

Finally, the girl noticed her and walked over.

Aiz looked up nervously, almost like a child waiting to be scolded, but when she saw the smile on Riveria's face, she smiled again.

"I'm home…Riveria."

"Yes. Welcome home, Aiz."

They both smiled broadly.

Their hair swayed slightly.

The breeze itself seemed to smile as it flowed between them.

Aiz · Wallenstein

BELONGS TO:	*Loki Familia*

RACE:	Human	**JOB:**	adventurer
DUNGEON RANGE:	twelfth floor	**WEAPON:**	shortsword

CURRENT WORTH:	320,000 valis

Status — Lv.1

STRENGTH:	C 609	**ENDURANCE:**	D 580
DEXTERITY:	B 798	**AGILITY:**	A 818
MAGIC:	H 100		

MAGIC:	Airiel	• Enchantment • Wind Element • Chant: "Awaken, Tempest"
SKILLS:	???	• ???

EQUIPMENT: Sword Yell

- Aiz's made-to-order weapon. A shortsword.
- Crafted by *Goibniu Familia*. 1,000,000 valis. After deciding to give her a custom weapon, Gareth, Finn, and Riveria covered most of the cost.
- Made of Damascus alloy sourced from the mining and steel manufacturing country Cham. Strong and sturdy. Heavy, but it boasts a cutting edge far above the weapons commonly wielded by lower-class adventurers. A steel sword with emphasis placed on attack power and endurance.
- The name is supposed to symbolize "sword's toast" in celebration of the girl's first custom weapon.

EQUIPMENT: Armor Dress—Loki Custom

- A prum armor dress modified to fit Loki's tastes.
- It reached its current state because of Aiz's growth and Loki's willingness to get it modified and updated.
- The girl doesn't know yet that when she exchanges her armor, her patron goddess will insist on each redesign revealing even more skin.
- Because it is a modification of existing armor, the value is comparatively cheap compared to custom gear at 42,500 valis.
- The white plates of the armor starting at her gauntlets are made of light metal and white wood, increasing the durability and decreasing the weight.

AIZ WALLENSTEIN

Afterword

This is the side story's ninth book, which takes place behind the scenes of the events in the main series' eighth book.

In terms of organization, unfortunately, the present-day segments have a bit of a feeling of skipping around, but if you read the main series' eighth book, I believe you will enjoy them even more.

With this book, part two is now complete.

Unlike part one, which featured the so-called strongest faction as they took on the Dungeon and all their various efforts, part two is mainly about shining a light on the main characters and their pasts. Since I wanted the final story to go to the main protagonist of the side story, allow me to finish this part here. (Though there are still characters here and there who I haven't covered yet.)

Personally, I'm always unsure how much of the side story's protagonist's backstory to reveal in the main series and how much to leave for this series. However, this time, as I was sketching it out, that past, or perhaps more so her bond with her familia, turned into the main topic of the story.

The frivolous goddess, the prum watching over her from a step removed, the heroic dwarf with his grandfatherly smile…and the high elf best described as her second mother. I think the collection of characters around the protagonist managed to make the main series' story much more vibrant.

In particular, the conflicted high elf really carried the story for me when I wasn't sure I could put it all into words. When she said "I love you," I was honestly surprised. I'm truly sorry for setting your character to be unmarried. In any case, it would be nice if there was another opportunity to write more episodes in the past where the protagonist and high elf show more emotion and are constantly bickering.

I'd like to move on to my thanks.

To my editor Takahashi, chief editor Kitamura, thank you for supporting me when I hit the brakes right before the goal. To Kiyo-taka Haimura, who gave the protagonist a different sort of cuteness in her past arc and as a village girl, my deep gratitude for providing such wonderful art despite the dreadful schedule the author stuck him with. To everyone who helped make this book happen, I extend my thanks. And also to all the readers, thank you for picking up my book.

Until the next book,
Thank you very much.
All the best.

Fujino Omori

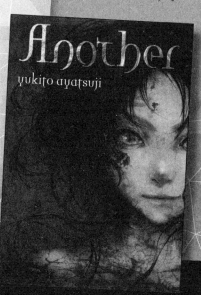

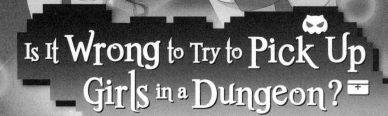